SO-ADU-426

Other titles by Jakob Arjouni

JAKOB ARJOUNI

CHEZ MAX

Translated from the
German by Anthea Bell

NO EXIT PRESS

First published in the UK by No Exit Press in 2009
P.O. Box 394, Harpenden, Herts, AL5 1XJ
www.noexit.co.uk

Supported by Arts Council England, through Grants for the Arts.

© Jakob Arjouni 2009

The right of Jakob Arjouni to be identified as the author of this work has been asserted
in accordance with the Copyright, Designs and Patents Act 1988.

All rights reserved. No part of this book may be reproduced, stored
in or introduced into a retrieval system, or transmitted, in any form
or by any means (electronic, mechanical, photocopying, recording or
otherwise) without the written permission of the publishers.

Any person who does any unauthorised act in relation to this publication
may be liable to criminal prosecution and civil claims for damages.

A CIP catalogue record for this book is available from the British
Library.

ISBN: 978-184243-258-7

2 4 6 8 10 9 7 5 3 1

Typeset by Avocet Typeset, Chilton, Aylesbury, Bucks
Printed and bound in Great Britain by J.H. Haynes Ltd, Yeovil, Somerset

In the Year 2064

Chapter 1

I was standing outside my restaurant – Chez Max, *cuisine allemande* – in the eleventh arrondissement of Paris, looking down the street to the building where Leon lived. Outside its sand-coloured façade, and looking like a gigantic tropical beetle, stood a shiny orange TEF. Such was the abbreviated English name of the Three Elements Fighter, the latest Eurosecurity task-force vehicle. It could drive on land, navigate in water and fly through the air, hence also its German name of BoWaLu, combining the first syllables in that language of *Boden*, land, *Wasser,* water, and *Luft*, air. As for the French, they called it an *Aireauterre*, the Italian name was something ending in *–oso*, I forget exactly what, but the rest of Europe just used the English term anyway.

The TEF had only been in use for six months, and the press, TV and government departments concerned were forever describing it as a technological miracle. Personally, knowing what life was like inside a TEF, I considered it a vehicle straight from hell. Its equipment consisted of several voice-operated machine guns; a mist-thrower; a flame-thrower; five explosive rockets (which also functioned under water as torpedoes); a laser beam that would cut through anything, even concrete; a super-sensitive directional microphone with a built-in translation computer capable of handling all known languages – including or perhaps particularly those now banned –

radar devices for locating human beings, chemicals, radioactivity and gases; as well as a TV, a dry shower, and a sandwich-vending machine offering a choice of three flavours: Parma ham, roasted vegetables with cheese, and kangaroo with pesto.

I knew all this so well because I and colleagues of mine from the Ashcroft agency had been sent on a TEF training course two months before. None of us knew exactly why, since our own activities never involved any direct contact with criminal or terrorist elements. But orders had come from Eurosecurity HQ: all security departments had to familiarise themselves with the operation and functions of the TEF.

After four days of this training programme I was able to drive the TEF a few kilometres, use the directional microphone to listen in on the conversation of two Finnish colleagues in the espresso lounge admiring our well-stacked female presenter, unintentionally fill the training hall with mist, and take a kangaroo sandwich out of the vending machine although I'd wanted Parma ham.

'You don't have to learn every little thing about operating the TEF,' the woman running our course explained. 'That would take several weeks of training. But if you happen to be near an incident during a TEF operation carried out by your colleagues from the Reality departments, it's in your own interests to know about the various weapons systems and what they can do. And of course you're duty bound to come to the aid of colleagues in an emergency. If the crew is in difficulties, and you can get inside the TEF, then you have to be capable of moving it out of the action zone.'

The training course leader spoke Serbo-Croat in a husky and to my mind very sexy voice, and I kept taking the simultaneous translation button out of my ear to listen to the original. Not that I knew a word of Serbo-Croat, so I missed the drift of half her lecture, but anyway I was certain that I would never try doing anything whatsoever with a TEF, let alone 'moving it out of the action zone'. Whatever that might mean.

I wasn't a Reality man, after all. I was an Ashcroft man. My sphere was crime prevention, not ongoing emergencies or dangerous situations.

But at that moment, as I stood outside my restaurant and looked down the street, I wasn't thinking of the rockets and machine guns hidden behind the orange bodywork; I was wondering, in some dismay, why they hadn't brought a normal police car to arrest a potential small-time drugs dealer. What would the neighbours think? The TEF made it look as if Leon were a serious offender or a terrorist. And I'd specially asked for discretion!

I felt my face going hot. This was wrong. And I hated it when things went wrong. On this occasion I was to some extent responsible, so I hated myself too. Because while it had been my job and my duty to inform on Leon, and I considered my job and my duty as an Ashcroft agent necessary to society and usually honourable, this time I'd rather have known as little as possible of the consequences of my actions. After all, I'd been acquainted with Leon for years, I had frequently welcomed him to Chez Max as a guest, I'd ended many evenings *tête-à-tête* with him over one of those squat bottles of Franconian wine, talking about women, life and love, and I'd often come close to regarding him as a friend.

And now this! They come rolling up in a TEF, causing an uproar. Over the next few weeks there'd be just one subject of conversation in the local streets and bars: could that cultivated, elegant, good-looking Leon, always ready with a joke, popular with women, be a murderer? A terrorist? A leading member of some fanatical group? Why else bring a TEF? Leon of all people, a man with so many natural advantages – everything about him was genuine, no cosmetic surgery on any part of his body, he hadn't even had his eyelashes lengthened – Leon, whose life seemed to consist solely of pleasure and amusement? On the other hand, what did he actually live on? He *said* he was a painter, and considering the number of women pretty enough to be artists' models who went in and out of his place, that could be true. But did we ever see him with a picture under his arm, or at least a blank canvas …?

I knew the story of Leon's artistic career. He had told me one night over our fourth bottle of Franconian wine. He had once been a painter – a real working painter, he still thought of himself as one, it was just that he couldn't get his pictures down on the canvas any more. I remembered being torn two ways that night. I'd never felt so close to Leon before, while at the same time I realised that I mustn't get too friendly. Because even at that time there was something about Leon to suggest that one day he'd come within the scope of the Ashcroft statutes, and then it would be the duty of the Ashcroft agent responsible for this part of the city to lay his conduct before the Examining Committee.

I looked from the TEF to the façades of the buildings to the right and left of it. Curtains were moving at the windows, faces disappeared and came into view again, families crowded together to look out, children pressed their noses to the window panes, old folk had drawn

10

chairs up to their window sills, and they were all waiting to see what that TEF was about to do.

I shook my head: Leon had simply had bad luck. Or he hadn't been able to exploit his good luck – perhaps it came to the same thing. And yet at first, if you believed his story, everything had gone so well for him. In his mid-twenties he graduated from the famous Warsaw College of Art, he went to Sicily for the climate and the light, moved into a studio in a former warehouse on Palermo harbour, and launched into the standard notion of an artist's life: painting, seaside walks, drinking wine, girls. After six months he had painted about thirty pictures; he went to see various galleries in Palermo and held his own first small exhibition. Naples and Rome followed, he slowly worked his way up, he met a rich woman who was an art dealer, fell in love with her, and had his work shown in a prestigious Zürich gallery. Meanwhile he kept on painting more pictures, clearly developing a style of his own, and he was soon considered a hot tip by those who knew his work. *Vodafone Art Magazine* described him as 'the most retro of present-day artists, in the best sense of that term. He boldly and refreshingly tackles the age-old still life genre, which should really have been a thing of the past by now, but he paints his apples and pears in so natural and sensuous a manner, with such a lavish wealth of colour, that you cannot tear yourself away from his pictures.' Inspired by the reception of his work, Leon sent photographs of it to galleries in Amsterdam, Berlin, Paris, London, attended private viewings, made contacts, got drunk every evening with major or minor figures in the art trade, and in spite of all this he was still painting at least a picture a week.

'I was sleeping only two or three hours a night, taking all the stimulants I could lay hands on – and at the time, as you know, it was still quite easy to get hold of synthetic cocaine. For a while those sods even thought of legalising it. Probably because they guessed that they couldn't keep people happy in the long run if there were no ways of having fun apart from *that*,' said Leon, nodding dismissively at the wine bottle.

I smiled. Leon's views and his way of expressing them amused me. But I automatically registered the fact that my neighbour had experience of drugs, and described the government as 'those sods'.

'Well, anyway, I all but killed myself, I took to the bottle like there was no tomorrow, I painted picture after picture – always those beautiful true-to-life pears, because that's what I was praised for, and I wasn't up for anything new, I didn't have the wherewithal for that – the wherewithal being peace and quiet, time, sobriety, and above all faith in myself.'

Leon glanced at me almost apologetically for a moment, then turned his head away and looked at the floor with distaste. As I watched him I felt a mixture of kindness and sympathy.

'In fact I was a little pile of famous shit. I wasn't an artist at all except for the deadlines I had to meet. And just at that point came the invitation to exhibit in one of the most important London galleries, Junowicz & Kleber. They wanted me to paint them an entire series. Twenty pictures. It was my big chance.'

Leon broke off, looked absently into space for a moment, then picked up the bottle and poured more wine for both of us, splashing it on the table.

'But I wasn't yet so washed up that I didn't know it. On the contrary: I knew perfectly well that here was one of the two or three moments in your life when the door opens briefly to show you a new, better, richer world. You have to run, you have to hurry to make the most of those moments, you have to stake everything. The main thing is to get in through that doorway, come what may – or out of it, as the case may be. But because I knew that so well, my chance very soon died on me. They'd given me six months to finish the series. I was drunk more or less round the clock for the first month, and in my few sober moments I threw away everything I'd done in my alcoholic delusions. Not that Junowicz & Kleber wanted anything special, just more apples and pears. But I suddenly thought it was time not simply to strike out in a new direction but to give them something out of the ordinary. I thought I had to reinvent myself from scratch. Because what was I at that time? A twenty-first century artist still painting fruit. And for all my arrogant mockery of the so-called avant garde, the sculptors who worked with gas, the designers of volcanic eruptions, the builders of fountains running with piss, God knows what else, I suddenly felt very insignificant beside them. They'd at least struck out in new directions, hadn't they? Tried to find new forms of expression, new levels of perception – or any pretentious way you like to put it. While there was I with oil paints, canvases, still lifes!'

Leon spat out the last words as if speaking of an enemy he hated. Then he picked up his glass, took a gulp, slammed it down on the table and stayed there, leaning forward, shoulders hunched, while his eyes wandered around the restaurant.

For a while I hardly dared to move. I watched Leon's motionless profile and waited for some sign from him. Finally I pulled myself together and said, cautiously, 'Well, personally I … I mean, I don't know much about art … but I like still lifes.'

'Oh yes?' said Leon slowly, sounding bored but also almost challenging as he turned to look at me. Under his gaze I felt I'd been caught in the act of something, though I didn't know what.

'Yes, really, I like them a lot,' I assured him, wondering if he thought I was making it up. 'I mean, look round this place.' And I indicated the room where we were sitting. 'This is my restaurant, I designed it myself, and what do you see on the walls?'

Leon briefly examined the pictures to left and right, framed posters of works by Matisse and Cézanne, and then looked at me incredulously for a moment.

'Yes,' he said then, nodded at me, and smiled faintly. 'Well, thanks.'

I almost said, 'Don't mention it,' purely as a reflex.

'I know my opinions aren't particularly ...'

'That's all right,' Leon interrupted me. 'Sorry.' After a moment he added, 'And I've always said that's what art is all about.' Without looking up, he gestured vaguely from the posters to me. 'But probably I'm just one of the many who are secretly pining to be famous in the colour supplements for fountains running with piss and all that.'

I had no idea what Leon was talking about. Once again I looked at his profile and didn't move a muscle myself. Not for fear of saying something wrong this time, however, but out of respect. Obviously Leon was fighting his own inner demons.

After a while I asked, 'So how did those six months go?'

Leon looked up as if he wasn't sure where he was. 'What?'

'The six months Junowicz & Kleber gave you to paint their series – what did you do?'

'Oh, that.' Leon picked up his glass of wine and drained

it. As he poured more, he said, 'After a month I stopped drinking, just like that, not another drop and then …' he smiled sardonically, 'then I reinvented myself. Painted my fruit as if painting fruit was the biggest joke in the world. Exaggerated the colours until they were sheer kitsch, put the fruit in rubbish bins or on paintings in galleries with visitors eating the fruit off the canvas, that sort of thing. I still had this mental picture of myself sitting with the Junowicz & Kleber people in the room behind the gallery, drinking champagne and making brilliant conversation. In my mind I was already so famous, my work was so highly thought of, that it struck me as extremely clever to make fun of my own stuff.'

He paused, and I took my chance to say quickly, 'Well, I can imagine it was very funny to have people eating the fruit.'

'Yes, exactly,' agreed Leon, nodding slightly, and I couldn't guess from his expression just how he really meant his 'Yes, exactly'. Then he added, 'But that doesn't matter. After another month I came to, and then I finally began working properly.'

Leon stopped and took a deep breath, as if he had to steel himself before he went on. 'And it worked. They wanted twenty pictures, three weeks later I had the first ten finished, and if I'm not much mistaken they were the best still lifes I ever painted. It was as if I had new eyes, as if I were suddenly seeing strong, living, startling colours again, and the arrangements and perspectives were so easy, it all came as naturally as if there wasn't any other way to put flowers or fruit down on the canvas. Friends who came to my studio couldn't take their eyes off those pictures. As if the fruit on my canvas had more juice in it, more magic about it, than the real fruit in their kitchens.

Or as if my pictures showed them, for the first time, what marvels Nature or God or whatever you like to call it creates. I had the feeling I'd found my way to the heart of it all. My pictures were the truth. So yes, they were only fruit and flowers, but the good Lord didn't start out with human desperation or couples locked in amorous frenzy, he began with single-cell organisms and photosynthesis – fish and leaves.'

For a moment Leon looked as if his words were little living creatures and he was watching them go, waiting expectantly to see if they'd be walking upright after this speech or slinking away, ashamed. Then his face suddenly changed, he cried angrily, 'Yes, I felt like God Almighty! Except that God didn't collapse after three days out of sheer terror that he couldn't keep the standard up. Or else he simply didn't realize what amazing stuff he was creating. As for me, I stood looking at my ten pictures, ten out of the twenty, I could already see the delighted faces of visitors to the gallery, I heard the critics' praise – and then suddenly, literally, I could hardly move any more. It began with numbness, first in my shoulders, then in my arms, and a few days later the shaking began. To this day the doctors haven't found out what's wrong. My muscles, my sinews, my brain – apparently they're all fine, but as soon as I pick up a brush or a pencil and get in front of a canvas, or just sit down with a pad of paper …' He raised his arm and mimed an uncontrollable tremor. 'No kidding. It's been like that for over fifteen years. I can write letters by hand, I can even thread a needle, but the moment I so much as think of drawing or painting … Oh, I still have my studio in Palermo, sometimes I fly there for an evening, sit by the sea, drink a couple of glasses of wine, act as if everything was normal, try to relax, to dream, I talk to a waiter I've known for the last fifteen years, I listen to the waves, and when the wine and the salty sea air have made me feel strong enough I pay the bill, and the waiter, who doesn't know anything about my block, wishes me good luck with my painting in his usual way. Then I go over to the studio in the old warehouse, just to sit with my easels and canvases for a while, breathing in the smell of paint and turpentine and smoking a cigarette or two. I have a cleaning lady who comes in once a month, there's no dust lying around, and it looks as if I'd painted my last picture only yesterday. So I sit there, I look around me, I smoke – everything's fine. Until I suddenly think of a flower or something like that. Usually it's flowers, always something really simple like daisies. And I see the flower more and more clearly in my mind's eye, I know just where to position it, how the shadow will fall, how I'll use the colours, and then I tell myself: no, just a simple sketch. No colours, no background, no shadowing. A quick drawing of a flower, the sort of thing you'd doodle while you're talking on the phone. After all, when I made a note of something yesterday I could still use a pencil ...'

I looked at the TEF and sighed. What a disaster! What Leon had told me that evening still seemed to me total proof of his artistic vocation, even more so at this moment, when he was probably already in handcuffs. The honesty of his description of his torments and his megalomania, his contempt for his own corrupt nature, the intensity he devoted to everything. And of course the pictures. I'd looked on the Internet next day, and through various roundabout links I'd finally tracked down two

17

reproductions of works by Leon Chechik in a Budapest gallery: 'Apples In Front of a Blue Sofa', and 'Almond Blossom Ecstasy'. I downloaded them to my smart three-by-three metres BTL original-reflection wall, and was fascinated. Sure enough, I'd never seen such fantastic almond blossom in real life. It positively exploded into the room out of a blue, sunny sky, it seemed as if I could touch the sea of flowers bathing me in a clear, pale pink light. I automatically thought of springtime, youth, being in love. I seemed to smell the sweet scent of the blossom. To think that an oil painting could do something like that! And because of the zero per cent additional lighting of the original-reflection wall, I could be sure that the colours in Budapest were at least as bright as those I saw here. How I would have liked to tell Leon next day what an impression his pictures had made on me! I even left 'Apples In Front of a Blue Sofa' as a permanent wall-saver; the sight of those apples rolling out of the basket as it tipped over, scattering apparently at random over the tiled floor and around the legs of the sofa, made me feel so calm and happy. But when Leon came into Chez Max that evening with a girlfriend, greeted the waiters as cheerfully as usual and joked about my Teutonic dive and German dumplings, I instantly dismissed the idea. For I knew what pain was hidden behind that façade. Any compliment paid to Leon, however heartfelt, would only remind him of fifteen years of artist's block. And a cheerful façade, I said to myself, is better than no cheerfulness at all.

Not that any of that, now I knew about Leon's smoking, kept me from emailing my colleagues in Palermo a few days later and mentioning in a tone of mild reproof that, as I had recently discovered, there was obviously still no difficulty in getting hold of cigarettes in their part of the world. There had been a total ban on smoking for over thirty years now. Anyone selling cigarettes faced jail, and for the last fifteen years smoking had also been a criminal offence for the consumer. However, I often heard that in the outlying regions of Europe – Sicily, eastern Russia, Turkey – smoking was still a part of everyday life for some sections of the population. Historically, Sicily had always been a problem when it came to enforcing pan-European laws and regulations, and I didn't expect any reaction to my email. But I wanted our colleagues at least to know that their lax attitude to cigarette smuggling did not go unnoticed. Only in passing, and to prevent it from looking as if I'd made the whole thing up to make myself look important, did I mention Leon's name. So I was all the more surprised when I had an answer from Palermo two weeks later, giving information about a gang of smugglers who were planning to set up a kind of chain of sales outlets for all banned drugs, from heroin to cigarettes, in Paris, Brussels and Amsterdam. And not only that: the painter Leon Chechik, whom I had mentioned, had been a close acquaintance of one of the gang bosses for about a year.

It wasn't the first attempt to distribute drugs on a large scale and systematically, so to speak – hence the term 'chain of sales outlets' – and it certainly wouldn't be the last, although such attempts had proved unsuccessful in north-west Europe for many years now. For one thing, because there was a much denser network of Ashcroft agents here than in the south and east, for another because of different mind-sets, or at least that was my own view, and many of my colleagues in Paris shared it.

At first the information from Palermo just made me

extra watchful for drug-dealing. Because where Leon was concerned, so I told myself after my first mild shock on hearing that he knew the gang boss, well, of course he had to find a source of supply for his cigarettes, and ultimately it didn't matter if he got them that way or from some old lady topping up her pension.

But the next week I saw Leon in Chez Max having a noticeably discreet conversation with a stranger. Although I'd have liked to overlook it or dismiss it as meaningless, all the alarm bells rang. Rather reluctantly, and with a queasy feeling in my guts, I took over serving from one of the waiters, went to the washroom and fitted the skin-coloured simultaneous translation button specially made for my inner ear into place – you could spot it only in bright light and from an almost impossible angle – and then I started working on Ashcroft business.

Even as I approached their table and caught a few sentences, my premonition that there was something fishy going on proved right. The stranger was speaking bad Italian with a strong accent.

My button translated. 'Gallery have to be small, not showy, same like with pictures – nothing trendy.'

'Maybe we can set up as specialists in charcoal drawings, something like that?' replied Leon.

'Yes, that good, that sound boring.'

Why wasn't he speaking his own language? After all, Leon had a simultaneous translation button too – you could get them for less than a thousand euros these days – and I knew he always carried his with him in his inside jacket pocket. Not such a small and sophisticated device as the buttons handed out to the Ashcroft people, of course; those could translate all languages and dialects faultlessly, even the texts of songs and the sound tracks of feature films. But the cheaper kinds were fine for a conversation in a restaurant, if you didn't mind about the grammatical niceties.

Or perhaps the stranger's mother tongue wasn't one of the Euro-Nineteen or Asia-Seven to which the European linguistic area had been restricted twenty-three years ago? They were the only languages allowed for civilian use by the simultaneous translation buttons. There remained certain tolerated languages – including Albanian, Catalan and Swiss German – plus the languages from what was known as the 'conflict area', Hebrew and the Arabic spoken in Palestine, and then there were the banned languages. All other forms of Arabic fell into that category, as well as all African and some Asian languages. Anyone using them on European soil faced a fine or imprisonment.

So what category might the stranger's mother tongue belong to? To my surprise, he turned out to speak almost faultless French.

'Hello, Max, how's it going?' Leon said in German. He had been born and brought up in Brussels, and spoke German, French and Italian as well as Flemish, a tolerated language. He went on in French. 'Meet my friend Benoît. He owns a gallery in Rome and he's going to open a branch in Paris. I'm going to run the place for him.'

I nodded and smiled at them both. 'Good idea.' And I added, to Benoît, 'If I may say so, I don't know anyone who knows as much about art and loves painting as fervently as Leon.'

Leon laughed. 'Oh, come off it! You sound like my old granny. And like my granny, you don't know any other painters. It's like me saying I've never met another German restaurateur who knows more than you about good food and a pleasant atmosphere. Of course, very likely there really isn't anyone better, but …'

I dismissed this and told Benoît, 'No comparisons are needed to do justice to something special.'

'But *cher monsieur*, that's a contradiction in terms,' objected Benoît in his lightly accented French, looking at me a little more keenly than this apparently innocuous situation warranted.

'Very well, then I'll tell you this: you don't have to be a connoisseur of roast venison to enjoy the venison we have on the menu today.'

'Aha!' cried Leon. 'Like I said, Max is the best! Gets his guest involved in some exchange of wisecracks, then sells him a steak that is as tough as old boots and filling up his freezer.'

They laughed, and then ordered fish soup Günter to start with, followed by the roast venison.

On the way to the kitchen, I could think of only one good reason why they weren't speaking French: they didn't want the other guests in the restaurant listening to them. While I served the fish soup, I took a couple of photos of Benoît with the camera in my contact lens.

Next morning the Ashcroft office in Rome told me that there was no gallery owner or art dealer by the name of Benoît in the city. Then I fed the photographs I'd taken into the Eurosecurity computer, and read all about Leon's acquaintance: *Abdel Aziz, Greater Southern area (Algerian or Moroccan), birthplace unknown, fishmonger, married, three children, two attempts to cross the sea to Europe, when arrested for the second time was sentenced to four years' hard labour in the mines of Namibia (Greater Far Southern area), last known place of residence Casablanca, has contacts with cannabis and tobacco growers.*

So he'd succeeded at the third attempt. I looked at the BTL wall showing 'Apples In Front of a Blue Sofa'. It was a fact that Leon's lifestyle was expensive, and he had sometimes said ruefully that without support from his family he'd have landed in the gutter long ago. But surely he couldn't be stupid enough to believe that doing business with this Abdel was the way to get out of that situation!

He could, though. That same week I listened in on parts of a conversation at the bar of Chez Max between Leon and one of his well-heeled girlfriends, in which he said among other things, 'In a month's time at the latest I'll be able to get you as much of it as you want.'

And the week after that, during my daily walks through the neighbourhood, I twice saw Leon and Abdel outside a brasserie in the Place Léon Blum with their heads together.

Next time Leon brought a girlfriend to Chez Max for dinner, I fixed a bug under the table, and next day, heavy at heart, I took the case to the Examining Committee. You could hear Leon on the recorder, speaking Flemish and saying things like, 'Cigarettes, hashish, even genuine coke – but that'll take a little longer.' And, 'I'm going to take over a gallery in the Place des Vosges and sell the usual tourist tat at the front of the shop.'

The Examining Committee did not for a moment doubt that Leon was on the point of committing a crime of moderate gravity, the duty lawyer raised hardly any objections, and sentence was passed swiftly and unanimously: three years in jail.

Four police officers in blue uniforms came out into the street through the open front door of the apartment building, with Leon in handcuffs between them. There was movement behind the windows in the buildings to left and right. Curtains were drawn further aside, arms signalled to people back inside the apartments, even more faces were glued to the panes. I instinctively took a step back. I felt like turning to disappear into the restaurant. But Leon might happen to see me, and I wanted to spare him that.

The police officers raised the side door of the TEF, pushed Leon in, three of them followed him while the fourth went round the vehicle to the driver's cab. At that moment I realized that they were going to drive right past me.

The engine started, humming quietly, and the TEF began to move. It slowly glided up the street towards Chez Max. Just before my place the street went round a bend, and the driver braked briefly. For a couple of seconds I could see Leon's head in the long armoured glass window. When he caught sight of me, a despairing smile flitted over his face, and he shrugged his shoulders as if to say, 'Sorry about this.'

I took care to look both surprised and encouraging. I'd have liked to call out, 'It must be some mistake! It'll all be cleared up!'

Just before the TEF picked up speed again, Leon raised his cuffed hands and waved slightly. I waved back.

When the TEF had disappeared around the next street corner, I turned and went into the restaurant. I sat down at Leon's favourite table with a glass and a bottle of plum schnapps. My heart was thudding and my throat felt dry. Surprisingly, I felt neither shame nor regret, only fear. I drank the first glass straight down. At the second or third glass, an odd thought occurred to me. I had never in my life smoked, I had never knowingly broken any law, but now I could imagine lighting a cigarette in Leon's honour.

That was nonsense, of course. Instead, I decided to make copies of his pictures and hang them over the bar instead of one of the Matisse posters. They would stay there, at least until Leon was free again. In three years' time or, with good conduct, two.

Chapter 2

The first Ashcroft offices had opened in 2029 in Paris, London, Berlin, Madrid, Rome and Moscow. By now a dense network covered Europe and North America, as well as parts of Asia. In the Greater Paris area alone there were twelve offices, plus our headquarters on the Place Sarkozy, where Chen and I had been allotted a room with a view of the Eiffel Tower.

The name Ashcroft derived from one of the last US Attorney Generals. There were two reasons why first Eurosecurity and then Asiasecurity had called their crime prevention departments, strange as it might seem, after an American politician who had been relatively quickly forgotten after the end of his four-year term in office in 2005. First, a name was required that would symbolize the beginning of efforts to set up a new world order, and it was generally considered that 11 September 2001 marked the birth of that new order. Second, the choice of an American name was a tribute to what had once been the most powerful country in the world, and one to which our new society undoubtedly owed a great deal. It was true that when the US went bankrupt, so to speak, turning from an industrial state into an agrarian society, it had lost a great deal of its importance, but no one had ever questioned its place as a part of Western civilization. That was why, in their annual governmental statements, the various European presidents said, using almost identical words: 'And I am also especially glad to address myself to our friends, sisters and brothers in North America.' Ashcroft was one of a whole series of once-famous Americans after whom organizations, squares, buildings or technical innovations had been named in Europe and China, so that the country's glorious past would not lapse into oblivion. Hence the Robert de Niro Suspension Bridge between Sicily and the Italian mainland, the Kurt Cobain Children's Holiday Camps, the Paris Hilton Dental Water Jets, and so on.

John Ashcroft himself had been known beyond the borders of the US for two things: first, for getting the bare breasts of the 'Spirit of Justice' statue in the reception area of his ministry covered up for moral and religious reasons, and second, of course, for his reflections on the legal possibility and social necessity of identifying and eliminating criminal elements before they actually got around to committing their crimes. Those reflections had been prompted by the moment, mentioned above, when the new world order came into being after the first great shock of the twenty-first century. On 11 September 2001 several of the spiritual forebears of today's Islamo-Fascist terrorist groups had hijacked four passenger aircraft, and in a kamikaze operation had flown them into the World Trade Center in New York and the Pentagon, killing over three thousand people and declaring war on the Western world and its values in the name of Muslim fanatics of all nations. As a result, of course, any number of measures to prevent similar attacks in the future were undertaken in the US and Europe by the secret services, the police and the military, but the vital theoretical new approach to the safeguarding of freedom and democracy came from Ashcroft. The words he is alleged to have uttered at the time, within the close circle around the US President, were still on the walls of almost every Ashcroft office toilet in their original English: *Let's crush the motherfuckers before they crush us.* Whether Ashcroft, who was well known for his deep Christian faith and strict morality – see the story about the statue – had ever really spoken the word *motherfucker* in the presence of the American president or anyone else is something that I have always doubted, but the gist was certainly appropriate, at least if by 'us' he meant a modern, liberal society in line with the ideas of the Enlightenment, constantly striving for progress not only in technology but also on a moral and spiritual level. A man who, let's say, pulled an insurance scam might not be crushing the whole of society, but he was spreading uneasiness and suspicion among at least some part of the population. And, as everyone knows, many small parts make up one large whole sooner or later. Averting that was the job of us Ashcroft women and men.

Ironically enough, it was John Ashcroft's ideas of preventative crime-fighting that, in their own time, were to lead indirectly to the downfall of the US as a world power. For the 9/11 assassins did not come from Los Angeles or Louisville, and their potential successors were not planning further terrorist attacks from some base in New Orleans. So if they were to be crushed first, the US had to invade foreign countries to get at them. First was Afghanistan (now part of the Greater South-Eastern Area), where the operation went relatively smoothly and successfully, if we leave aside the fact that the man behind the assassins, Osama bin Laden, the most important of the radical Muslim leaders, was not captured despite the best efforts of the ultra-modern US army and any number of special task forces. (Incidentally, we still feel the after-effects of this failure today: bin Laden's body was never found either, and so he became a sort of immortal prophet in the religious fantasies of the terrorist groups that we regularly confronted. Only last month I had brought a sympathizer with the potential for providing a terrorist hide-out before the Examining Committee, after noticing from my balcony that he had hung a poster of bin Laden in his living-room.)

But what, as everyone knows, really broke the US was the subsequent war against Saddam Hussein's Iraq, now part of the Greater Middle-Eastern Area. Ashcroft's ideas were especially prominent in providing the theoretical and moral framework for the war, since up to that point Iraq posed no threat to the United States. However, of course there were Islamist leaders and groups in Iraq who *could* have become a threat at some point, and if you looked at it that way, it was quite right in the Ashcroftian sense to bring the country under control as a preventative measure.

But a consequence of the American victory over Saddam's army that had not been foreseen – and in my view it couldn't logically have been foreseen – was the massive influx into Iraq of opponents of the US from all over the world, flooding in to raise hell for the occupying forces with their sniping and suicide bombings. The rest is history. The mightiest army in the world was worn down over the years in bloody skirmishes, the duties of occupation, and a vain attempt to get the Iraqis to recognize them as saviours who had brought democracy to the country. All the same, the US government stuck to its plan to usher in a new order and thus a lasting peace in Iraq and the entire Middle East of the time, while the two other great powers, China and Europe, concentrated entirely on economic progress. The Franco–Chinese Treaty of Hong Kong followed, and a little later the Euro-Chinese Confederation, which started by cancelling all loans to the exhausted and deeply indebted US and soon afterwards was in a position, as it were, to buy up the whole of North America.

Still feeling the force of the American failure in the Middle East, the Confederation undertook the construction of a fence around the world as the logical implementation of Ashcroftian ideas, excluding most potential enemies of our liberal and democratic society once and for all. Where US governments had gone on working, as one might say, to resocialize the problem zones of the world by waging war, hunting down dictators, holding elections and hoping for values to change in favour of democracy and the free market economy, the Confederation really did 'crush the motherfuckers'. At the same time as the Fence was being built, the armies of Europe and China began disarming the rest of the world. There followed the Great Wars of Liberation, lasting just under five years, at the end of which all military equipment in the southern hemisphere was either destroyed or rendered non-viable, and the Fence was completed. The Fence divided the world for all time, roughly speaking, into areas of progress and regress – or, at least, stagnation, although conditions in the two parts could not, of course, be described as one hundred per cent progressive or regressive. But the general gist was correct, and without the Fence the radical elements of the Second World would long ago have dragged us down into their own abyss of primitive religion, the glorification of violence, and contempt for anything different – if only because at some point we would have been ready to confront them, trying perhaps

Jakob Arjouni

to negotiate with them, to compromise, to give up our own freedom in the vague hope of peace. But you don't discuss with fanatics, and there are some negotiating tables where you have lost as soon as you sit down at them. Let them tear each other to pieces, and so indeed they did.

It was a shame that Ashcroft was to know no more of the fruits of his ideas than the American failure in Iraq. The grand old man of crime prevention had died in his home state of Missouri long before the erection of the Fence, and even longer before the first offices named after him were opened.

But perhaps his strict religious faith means that the good Lord sometimes lets him take a look at the world below. If so, Ashcroft could feel justifiably proud to see the Western world protected from dangers abroad and kept in order at home on the basis of his ideas. I won't go so far as some and claim that in the twenty-first century we, the heirs of Voltaire, Mozart, Picasso, owed not just our intellectual survival but our survival *tout court*, as the French say, solely to John Ashcroft, but the notion cannot be dismissed out of hand. I for one could only welcome the efforts of our Mental Health Department, MHD for short, to establish Ashcroft in the public mind as one of the spiritual fathers of the modern world. It's true that the population at large still regarded Ashcroft agents as mere informers, better avoided if you had identified them as what they were. But all that was to change. The papers outlining the strategy for that change were already in the Eurosecurity pigeon-holes. The plan was to bring general mobilization to bear to transform our society into a single great Ashcroft organism, in which everyone would have so much social and moral responsibility for himself and his fellow women and men that, with such a dense network

32

of actively public-spirited feeling, crime would simply no longer be possible. With that end in view, MHD was supplying the music and fashion media with cool, witty quotations from Ashcroft, anecdotes about him, and working hard to get T-shirts with his picture on them into the clothes stores where mostly young people shopped. Perhaps the time wasn't ripe for that yet, but some day Ashcroft would take his place on the clothes rails beside Che Guevara and Elvis, I didn't doubt that for a moment.

Two days after Leon's arrest, I met Chen in our room at Ashcroft Central Office, as I did every Friday. I was feeling terrible. Something in me must have snapped when Leon was taken away before my very eyes. Even though I knew better, I felt like a traitor. For the first time in over fifteen years as an Ashcroft man, I seriously doubted the point of it all, and kept asking myself why I hadn't turned a blind eye to Leon's smoking. There'd have been no problem about that; smoking, after all, was one of those crimes that didn't really endanger anyone or anything. But I was set on showing our Sicilian colleagues that the Ashcroft outfit had a really tough guy here in Paris, right on the ball. *I have recently discovered that there is obviously still no difficulty in getting hold of cigarettes in your part of the world.*

But I knew very well that lately I'd been anything but tough and right on the ball. On the contrary, I'd been neglecting my Ashcroft duties for my work at Chez Max and my increasingly desperate search for a woman to share my life with. That was probably why I'd passed my information on to the Sicilians. If I'd been informing on a terrorist every week, I'd hardly have thought it worth reporting an acquaintance's occasional indulgence in cigarettes. Instead, the last four weeks had come up with only the young man whose bin Laden poster had happened to catch my eye from my balcony.

But could I have expected the message I sent to Sicily to have such consequences? Of course not. All the same, I still felt guilty.

And now Chen. In my present frame of mind, he was about the last person I wanted to see. Still less, however, had I wanted to cancel our appointment and thus show that something wasn't quite right. I just hoped we'd get through our meeting without any mention of Leon. I could hardly have suppressed the urge to justify myself, and there was no doubt at all that Chen would have made use of that to stage an intellectual bloodbath. Remarks about friendship, trust, loyalty, the duties of an Ashcroft agent, social responsibility, priorities, and conscience would all have been left lying on the field of battle, charred, mutilated and smeared with blood, while Chen marched up and down waving flags and beating drums of vanity, cowardice, profit and heartlessness.

So I firmly made up my mind to meet any provocation offered by Chen over Leon's arrest with total indifference. I just wanted to get home quickly.

As I sat at the desk waiting for Chen to join me so that we could exchange our news on suspicious factors and any overlapping operations in our area, he was standing at the window with a plastic container of noodles and a fork, his back turned to me, looking out at the Eiffel Tower. With his mouth half full, he said: 'People are swine, it's always been like that, it always will be, and the world they create is a pig of a world. No laser projection of artificial rainbows on the sky or any other new technological crap is going to change that.'

He shovelled the next forkful of noodles into his mouth and smacked his lips noisily as he munched. Nothing interested me less at that moment than another of Chen's misanthropic tirades, but all the same I thought: I really ought to tell him I can't help agreeing, when I see and hear him eating like that. Humanity hasn't made much progress since we were crouching in caves devouring wild animals.

As Ashcroft agents, we'd been sharing responsibility for Quadrate Three of the eleventh arrondissement in Paris for over four years, we met once or twice a week, and Chen nearly always brought some item of fast food with him, consuming it in a way that made me wonder whether he'd had any parents or guardians as a child. But I didn't have the courage to say anything to Chen about it. Yet, even if it had come to a real quarrel I'd have had nothing to fear. Chen wasn't popular with our Ashcroft colleagues, and even our boss, Commander Youssef, a man who normally refrained from expressing personal opinions, had let it slip a couple of times that Chen got on his nerves with his sarcasm, his coarse language and constant air of superiority.

But I wasn't thinking of any official consequences that disagreement within an Ashcroft team might have, I was just thinking of Chen's possible retorts. He might say, 'Oh, does the way I eat bother you? You ought to hear me fart – and smell me too!' (And if I knew Chen, he would indeed fart as often as possible from then on.) Or perhaps, 'Oh, sweetie, I'm ever so sorry! I do realize I can't quite emulate the table manners of the posh customers in your restaurant who stuff their faces with birds' tongues in oyster sauce!' (He hardly ever missed an opportunity of referring to the high prices at Chez Max and the rather fashionable, slightly arty customers who came there). Or then again he might say (in German), '*Ach, mein Führer!*' and then (reverting to French), 'So sorry, but it's my race. We Asians guzzle like pigs – it's in the genes, see? I do see that's bound to upset a refined Aryan who'd sooner bump people off than slurp his soup. Oh dear, are you sending me to the gas chamber now, *mein Führer?*'

There were no limits to Chen's wealth of invention when he wanted to offend someone. He could take half an ingredient and turn it into an entire menu of the most varied insults in no time at all. I was always on my guard with him. If the espresso from the Ashcroft cafeteria in the building was a thin, watery brew yet again, I refrained from comment so as not to give Chen another chance of denouncing the spoilt, snooty ways of the world in general and his pernickety German colleague in partic-ular. For similar reasons, I took care not to keep my desk too tidy, or polish my shoes before going to the office, or wipe Chen's hairs out of the dirty wash-basin too often. Similarly, as far as possible I avoided giving my own opinion on any subject, showing emotions, or expressing any serious wish. The more anything mattered to someone, the keener Chen was to pounce on it, pick it to pieces and make it look ridiculous. Once, over two years ago, I had announced at the office, bubbling over with happiness, that I was in love. She was a new assistant in the kitchen at Chez Max, and it didn't take Chen ten minutes to paint a picture, by dint of a few questions and comments, of an ambitious young future head chef for whom Chez Max was just the right step up on the ladder of her career. 'Or why do you think she'd want anything to do with a man twenty years older than she is? You still look quite good for your age, but you're more of a quite good-looking father figure.'

What was so nasty about this, in retrospect, was that it turned out exactly as he'd predicted. I gave Yasmin the job of second chef six months later – causing some discontent among the rest of the staff who had been there longer, because Yasmin's talent for making sauces and assessing the right cooking time was not by any means entirely beyond reproach – and then three months after that a large hotel near the Palais Royal snapped her up from under my nose. About two weeks later she wrote to me saying that her new job as section chef for soups and starters in the restaurant, which boasted two hundred covers, left her hardly any time for private life; on the other hand, she said, her relationship with me was 'too important' to her to 'suffer, perhaps, from being relegated to the sidelines', so she would like 'a kind of time out' until she had established herself in her new job. I never heard any more from her.

And that was probably the main problem with Chen: he was usually right. As an Ashcroft agent, he was the best I'd met in over fifteen years of crime prevention at spotting crimes before they were committed. If he'd only been barking up the wrong tree a few more times in the last four years, I'm sure I'd have felt braver about disagreeing with his generally sweeping and simplistic judgements and analyses. No doubts of any kind ever seemed to trouble him. I often felt like saying: 'You really do over-simplify. As if everyone functioned by the book, in exactly the same way. But we're all different, we're very complicated and full of surprises. Take a closer look for once.' However, I knew what Chen would say to that. 'My job is preventing crime, not exploring the human psyche. And every idiot thinks he has an amazingly complex interior life. But then he feels ravenously hungry, he sees his neighbour with a piece of meat and strikes him dead. And of course he'll come up with some very subtle reasons for it.'

Several times I'd been on the point of asking Commander Youssef to transfer me to another district. What had held me back so far was first, of course, the prospect of having to close down Chez Max and start all over again with a new restaurant somewhere else, and second the admission of defeat that such a request would have implied. Because they hadn't put me and Chen together as a team by pure chance. Even then, his reputation as a master in spotting potential crimes in advance and an absolute arsehole into the bargain was legendary. I, by way of contrast, was regarded as a quiet force, courteous, unassuming, kindly, and completely incorruptible. Nothing seemed able to rattle me, so they thought I was the right man to crack the Chen problem on the human level. If he had an ever-friendly character just quietly murmuring away beside him, perhaps eventually he might simply get bored with terrorizing people. And that's what I thought myself at the start: carry on if you want to, I mentally addressed him, time and patience are on my side, and the day will come when you've worked it all off. As if he were an annoying child. Except that children who act like that are usually seeking attention from other people, whereas Chen seemed perfectly happy with just himself. I can't count the times I'd heard his angry voice already raised as I went along the corridor to our room, only to realize with annoyance when I went in that he was on his own.

'… those hypocritical bastards! "Oh, there's a man in our cellar! Not that we want to get him into trouble, but perhaps he needs help ..." Aha, and what do you know, here comes dear nice Max!'

'Good day, Chen.'

'Wow, good *day,* Che-e-en! More like good morning to you! My word, dear Max has bags under his eyes too! Been having it off with the sexomat all night long?' He circled his hips provocatively. 'Oooh, aaah – come on, you pale, pretty leisure-time photographer with the A1 tits straight out of the catalogue, I'm going to do you doggy-style and call you a slag...'

'That's okay, Chen.'

'What's okay?'

I didn't answer, just put my briefcase on the desk and started unbuttoning my trench coat.

'Oh, do tell me what's okay. Is *anything* okay? Something okay would be a nice change. Well? You can't just burst in here saying "That's okay," and stop at that. Let's hear it – what's okay?'

'Oh, Chen!' I sighed. 'You're in a bad mood, and I get it, that's all I meant.'

'Oh, so it's "okay" for you if you just get something. Well, I don't know. Me, I keep getting things, I really get just about everything except space travel and physics and all that crap – but do I always think it's "okay"? There's far too much fuss made about getting things anyway. Enlightenment and all that shit. I mean, everyone thinks...' here Chen adopted a naïve, squeaky tone like a small child, 'everyone thinks, ooh, if I'm going to improve anything I must get it first, getting things is ever so subtle, look at little me, aren't I wonderful? Yup, the fact is,' he concluded, scratching his head like a monkey, 'getting things is all you need to do.'

'Look, Chen, I have no idea what you're talking about.'

'Well, human beings, of course, affinities, systems, relationships – the whole filthy world. You were probably thinking of cooking sauerkraut.'

And so on. When Chen was in the mood for it he would carry on with this verbal cut-and-thrust until I put my trench coat on again and left. At our next meeting he sometimes apologized for his behaviour, sometimes he didn't.

In fact the pitiful state of the world and the stupid, brutish nature of human beings and their leaders were among Chen's favourite subjects. In our early weeks working together, that had both surprised and shaken me. After all, Chen was an Ashcroft man, and thus part of Eurosecurity. We were doing our bit to defend the values and interests of Europe in Quadrate Three of the eleventh arrondissement. We were – as the Ashcroft oath put it – 'duty bound to show moral, spiritual and active devotion to the government and its laws.' Chen could afford to talk the way he did only because his contribution to the statistics of crime prevention in the heart of Paris was regularly sensational. Of course some of our colleagues muttered privately that in the 'noodle-soup alleys' frequented by Chen, there was no difficulty in foreseeing a crime a week, but I considered that plain racism.

In the first few years after the Peking Treaty of 2038, which had both eased travel between China and Europe and greatly increased the annual quota of legal immigration, over a million Chinese had moved to the Greater Paris area. Of course many illegal immigrants also arrived and stayed, but most immigrants had the right papers. Generally they settled in the suburbs, but there were also several parts of the city centre where the population was now ninety per cent Chinese, or European of Chinese descent. The dividing line between Chinatown Voltaire and the part of the eleventh arrondissement where the population was mainly white ran through the quadrate that Chen and I covered. Apart from the fact that I had been operating successfully in my own area there for over fifteen years and had set up ideal cover in the form of Chez Max, it had been only natural to recruit Chen for surveillance of the Chinese area because of his family origins and his knowledge of Mandarin. He worked there as a municipal gardener tending public parks, trees and flowerboxes. The job meant that he was out of doors most of the time, could stand around observing things without arousing any suspicion, dropped easily into conversation with passers by on innocuous subjects such as flower varieties or the height of hedges, and never needed to come up with an explanation if he thought it a good idea to take a closer look at an apartment or a cellar. There was always a handy tree with an allegedly diseased crown that had to be inspected from the balcony or window of the apartment concerned, or Chen might invent an under-ground watercourse to be laid out for the shrubs in the nearby playground: he had to examine the floor of the suspect cellar with a special instrument, he said, to decide just where the watercourse would run.

In my own view, Chen's success as an Ashcroft agent was based on excellent cover, familiarity with the customs and habits of the local inhabitants, his special gift for observation, his intelligence, and what, when I thought of his frequently unpleasant and contemptuous assessment of other people, was a remarkable ability to empathize.

In addition, it had been statistically proven that in districts with a high percentage of Chinese inhabitants, on average just as many crimes of just the same kinds were committed as in socio-economically comparable white areas. And since the population of Chinatown Voltaire consisted largely of sole traders, white-collar workers, craftsmen, restaurateurs, lawyers, doctors and artists, the crimes detected by Chen in advance were mainly cases of insurance and tax fraud, child abuse, rape, blackmail and murder motivated by avarice or jealous rage. What envious colleagues said about him was thus nonsense in every way. On the contrary: if there was one weak point in Chen's activity as an Ashcroft agent, and this had struck me over and over again during the years we'd been working together, it was that in his advance detection work the crimes usual in immigrant quarters, those that our colleagues had in mind when they tried to smear his success rate, were hardly ever committed. Theft, extortion and gambling were thin on the ground, as were drug-related crimes – although the weakness of many Chinese for cigarettes was notorious, and smoking was still regarded as a mere peccadillo in China. And there was little illegal immigration or terrorist propaganda. So little, in fact, that anyone other than Super-Chen would probably long ago have laid himself open to suspicion of taking bribes or actually conniving in crime. For of course Chinatown Voltaire had its gangs of young tearaways, its drug dealers, people-smugglers and radical political activists. It almost seemed as if Chen wanted to portray his area of operations in a certain light – oddly enough, as I sometimes reflected in surprise, in the gentle, all-enveloping light of the upper middle class that he liked to deride at the top of his voice. A light that blurred the lines.

'… let them think everything's fine for another few days. Sure, we can project rainbows on the sky! Next thing you know we'll be reconstructing the Lord God himself, giving him a bit more authority and assertiveness, and then all that love-your-neighbour stuff will work properly at last.'

Chen raised the plastic container to his mouth and slurped up what was left of the sauce. I looked out of the window. I wished I could have listened out of the window too.

Scarcely three hundred metres away, the Eiffel Tower rose against the radiant blue of the spring sky. Muted shouting and laughter floated up from the Champ de Mars. Soon the moment would come. The event had been announced in all the media weeks ago: an artificial rainbow to arch above the Eiffel Tower. Technically that was nothing very new; in principle it worked just like the Cinema In The Sky that had existed for years now. The difference was that films could be shown on Cinema In The Sky only after dark, so that after the first flush of enthusiasm its popularity with the public had waned relatively quickly. Senior citizens and families with children soon found it far from pleasant to have the night sky turned into a single huge cinema screen every other summer evening. You did need to wear headphones to hear the sound track, but groups of spectators on balconies and in roof gardens still made so much noise that those who weren't watching the film could hardly hope to get to sleep until it finished. And then there was the light problem. Although the regional departments of Cinema In The Sky tried to pick films that suited the evening atmosphere, almost every movie had some scenes set in daylight out of doors, and often bathed an entire city or a country area in bright sunlight for minutes on end at eleven at night. The one way to escape the show was to close your windows and shutters in the middle of summer. Only in Spain had Cinema In The Sky enjoyed unbroken popularity for years. By dint of collecting signatures on petitions and staging public protests, the people in many towns there had even managed to get the films shown later, on the grounds that if they began at nine or ten in the evening hardly anyone would get to eat an evening meal. However, in the rest of Europe the Cinema In The Sky technology was now used only on special and usually serious occasions, for instance for important government announcements or the promulgation of new laws. As a means of entertainment and amusement it had largely lapsed into oblivion. That had to be the explanation for why so many Parisians were wild with excitement at the prospect of seeing an artificial rainbow over the city. Since six in the morning, people had been queuing for tickets to the great Fête Arc-en-Ciel which was to begin in half an hour's time under the Eiffel Tower and on the Champ de Mars, with the appearance of the rainbow and a performance by the Veterans' Band of the Border Guards. After that there would be speeches by several members of the Brussels government, as well as the Governor of France and the Mayor of Paris, followed by an aerial ballet performed by the famous Danone School of Dance from Montpellier, a TEF air show, and finally the opening of the Peace Buffet, which was one and a half kilometres long. For the rainbow was to symbolize, not least, Europe's progress from the building of the Fence and the Wars of Liberation into an ever more peaceful and better future in which life would be more and more worth living.

Without taking my eyes off the Eiffel Tower I said, in the patient and forbearing tone that I had determined to adopt for this meeting, 'Well, it'll be nice if the rainbow makes a few people happy.'

'Why will it be nice? I've known people who were made happy by beating their own children or gunning someone down.'

'Oh, Chen …' I sighed. 'That's nonsense. It didn't make them happy. Such people are sick. And even if it did make them happy, surely it's better for them to look at a rainbow.'

'You mean that's the choice? Gunning someone down or the rainbow? Maybe you're right. Many might see it that way. But I'm afraid most wouldn't want to commit themselves. And then again: just how brutal is it, looking at a rainbow when someone's snuffing it next door?'

Oh please, I thought, not that stupid stuff again. Sometimes Chen really did talk like a depressive sixteen-year-old, or a rabble-rouser at some provincial university. After four years it was still a mystery to me how a man of his intelligence could seriously come out with such hollow, outmoded ideas. He probably just wanted to provoke me, but sometimes he took a tone that made me feel that these were the only ideas he really believed in.

Maintaining my equable tone, I replied: 'No one will be snuffing it next door. What ideas you think up! Far from it. We've never had it so good. There's enough food to eat – and although that doesn't interest you, it's quality food – there's enough work, nature is healthy, our seas are clean, medicine is making progress all the time, soon we'll have an average life expectancy of a hundred, and according to the latest surveys seventy per cent of the population consider themselves happy.'

Chen looked expressionlessly at me for a moment, shrugged his shoulders, threw the empty plastic container into the waste paper basket and the fork into the wash-basin and said, sounding bored, 'I don't know if you're suffering from some kind of partial memory loss. Let me remind you that there's no question that there is not enough food in many areas behind the Fence, let alone "quality food".'

I felt the blood drain from my face. And I'd firmly determined not to let that happen in front of him today. Because Chen registered everything, and once he'd exposed my emotions he'd find it easy to hit me below the belt, if that was what he wanted to do, by the mention of Leon's arrest, enriched by a wealth of allusions. And in fact I'd been surprised that he didn't bring the subject up as soon as we were in the office together. 'Well, my dear Max, busy protecting society again? Hauling a friend in front of the Examining Committee because he wanted to buy cigarettes! I suppose we all have our priorities.'

I'd been prepared for that, but not for what he'd just said. Because in spite of his unconcealed dislike of many aspects of present conditions, during the years we'd worked together Chen had seldom overstepped a certain line, and then only when he was drunk – which had always given me a good reason to forget the incident quickly. But the mere mention of certain global subjects ought to make me report him to Commander Youssef. Of course we could talk about the Fence – in fact we had to, since after all it was one of the duties of an Ashcroft agent to make sure it was maintained in good order and no one could get over it, and we did that by tracking down organizations that aimed to destroy it. A line had to be drawn, all the same. It wasn't laid down in law or stipulated in any decree, but everyone knew it. Commander

Youssef had once put it this way in a lecture that he gave in-house: we had to think of the regions beyond the Fence as we thought of the Moon – politically speaking, there was just as little to be discussed. The Moon couldn't be liberated either, and no one was doing it any wrong. In the course of an Ashcroft investigation we could, of course, pretend to express certain views to a suspect for the purpose of gathering evidence, but otherwise the rule was: anything said about the regions beyond the Fence, other than the geographical facts, counted as propaganda and an attack on our Euro-Asian community of values.

That was the official formula in the Civil Code: 'Attacks on our Euro-Asian community of values.' Quite a lot could come under that heading, and sometimes even I wondered if the point couldn't have been made a little more precisely. In most cases it depended on your personal judgement whether something was an attack or just thoughtless talk. Of course I knew that behind it all was the aim of bringing the population up to have a sense of responsibility, motivating citizens to think about what they did and said and examine it, instead of just stolidly keeping the rules. But an Ashcroft agent could sometimes find himself floundering. For instance, was my green-grocer's casually ironic throwaway remark about 'A1 bananas from sunny Nantes' just a joke, or could it be seen as the beginnings of a verbal attack on the Euro-Asian community of values? Because of course Nantes was only one of the ports where fruits and other produce from South America and Africa arrived. But as both Africa and large parts of south America lay beyond the Fence, the only way of describing the origin of the bananas was by their last point of delivery, in this case the northern French port of Nantes with its heavy average rainfall.

Then there was the lady who lived next door to me and mentioned her Senegalese grandfather whose native land she'd so much like to visit, adding bitterly that unfortunately Senegal was now under water, so she supposed her distant relations had evolved into fish. It was a fact that on official maps, like those shown on the TV news, all areas beyond the fence were plain blue, as if they were part of the oceans.

But talk about an alleged lack of food among the population living beyond the Fence – without a doubt, that was a deliberate attack on our joint Euro-Asian values. Because even if, on closer examination, living conditions there might be approaching some critical point or other, claiming hunger was ridiculous. After all, everyone knew that almost all our nutritional requirements were supplied by goods from South America, Africa and Asia. North America did make a contribution, but few thought much of its predominantly symbolic significance. Since the bankrupt USA had been excluded from Europe, European governments had always tried to point out the importance of North America as a supplier of grain and meat to the Euro-Asian world, for one thing in order to justify, to their own people, the huge subsidies granted annually to US agriculture, for another to encourage a sense of community with our 'poor relation' Uncle Sam overseas. The logic of this increasingly escaped most Euro-Asians of the younger generation.

But being poor – or at least not as prosperous as the Euro-Asian community – didn't mean starving, not by a long way. Neither in North America nor in the areas commonly known as 'the fluid regions' because they were shown in blue. On the contrary, even during the war or during periods of great over-population, farmers and herdsmen had naturally always been the last to run short of food. So what Chen had said was pure propaganda. Dangerous, too. I had no idea what was bugging him to make him say such a thing to me.

Chen had crossed his arms and was watching me with a lurking half-smile. I didn't know where to look. Why was he displaying such smug self-satisfaction now of all times? I felt like getting to my feet and saying, 'Right, I'm going to visit Commander Youssef and tell him we have a terrorist cell here in Ashcroft Central Office.' Just to see Chen's face.

At that very moment his mouth stretched in a genuine grin, and he shook his head. 'Sometimes I really wonder why they ever recruited you as an Ashcroft agent. You're easier to see through than my seven-year-old niece. But probably that's just why you're successful. No one can imagine that there's anything shady about you. Right now you're thinking of going to our superior officer. And what do you think I'll tell him myself?'

I noticed my nostrils beginning to twitch nervously.

'Chen, normally it would be my duty ...'

'Oh, come on! I'll tell you what your duty is: familiarizing yourself with the arguments of international terrorists and the way they talk. How are you ever going to convict anyone or uncover a secret operation if you turn as pale as a Jesus-date the first time someone questions your nice little Chez Max world?'

I had to pull myself together so as not to let fly childishly. This wasn't the first time Chen had described me as a Jesus-date, and a woman I'd been courting a few months ago, with flowers and chocolates and all the rest of it, had made the same comparison the last time we met. Since North America, except for New York and the

Los Angeles Museum of Post-Modern Life, had become an almost entirely agricultural area, the traditional Christian faith, already widespread there anyway, had developed into a kind of state religion among the population. Only the European government and its military presence in the area had so far prevented the New Testament from being adopted as the Civil Code between Kentucky and Death Valley. Various fundamentalist American groups were all the keener on sending missionaries to preach to the European population, putting pressure on our government over the legal status of the Bible, trying to get it to make a confession of faith. Armies of half-veiled young women preaching the Gospel were regularly sent across the Atlantic. You saw them swamping pedestrian zones, singing and praying, and they were known for their rather abstracted smiles and the composure that they showed, ranging from brave to slightly dogged, when their beliefs didn't meet with a suitably serious response. Because of the veils, sunlight seldom reached their faces, most of which were white, and if one of these young missionaries lifted her veil during a conversation designed to convert you, her skin was usually translucent with a faint tinge of pink. When such girls turned pale or blushed, it was extremely obvious, especially as the change was so very distinct from their otherwise sternly controlled and almost entirely unemotional facial expressions. One of the favourite slogans of these preachers of the faith, who concentrated on the young people of Europe in particular and were often not much older than twenty themselves, was: 'I'm dating Jesus.' All this had led to the coining of the expressions 'pale (or red) as a Jesus-date', which had now become part of the colloquial language.

I cleared my throat and slowly and carefully clasped my hands on the table.

'Maybe I'm just worrying. After all, not everyone in these offices knows you as well as I do, and I'm pretty sure few are as kindly disposed to you. I'm not shocked by what you said – nothing *you* say is going to shock me very easily – only by the idea that you might repeat such nonsense in front of one of our colleagues, someone who may be just waiting for a chance to get back at that arrogant arsehole Chen.'

To my surprise, he laughed. 'That was fun, right? Calling me an arrogant arsehole with the best of intentions.'

'Oh. Chen.' I closed my eyes briefly, as if exhausted. 'Not everyone relishes strong language as much as you do. If I wanted to insult you, believe me, I'd know how to go about it more subtly than that.'

'Sure, you'd know how to go about it if you wanted to …' He had pursed his lips and was batting his eyelids in a silly way like a parody of a prim and proper young girl. 'Well, let's hope I understand what you're talking about if you're going to be so subtle about it. Maybe you're insulting me the whole time and I'm so thick I just think: wow, there goes Max, what a refined fellow he is, always well-behaved, ever so pernickety, never says a bad word … could he be beating the crap out of me and I just don't notice?'

Chen beamed cheerfully at me. If anyone had taken a photo of him, people seeing it at some future date would very likely have come to the conclusion that he had just that moment announced his engagement, or something similar.

I looked out of the window at the Eiffel Tower, and all

at once a deep sense of kinship with the building came over me. As if I were at a party, surrounded by complete strangers, and suddenly saw a familiar, beloved face. For a moment the Tower seemed to free me from the fact that I had to sit in an office with a poisonous dwarf like Chen. And immediately I thought of Leon. He would have understood how I felt. I could have said to him, 'The Tower is over a hundred and fifty years old and it still makes an architectural and aesthetic statement – isn't it a wonderful, uplifting thought to be part of a creation capable of erecting such a mighty building with all its beauty and elegance?'

And Leon, as a sensitive artist, would have known exactly what I meant.

'Right,' I said, looking at the floor and nodding in an understanding way. 'I suppose that brings down the curtain on our weekly performance. Can we get around to discussing our operations now, or do you want to go on familiarizing me with the arguments of international terrorists and the way they talk a bit longer?'

'Tut-tut-tut.' Chen clicked his tongue in a friendly manner. 'No sarcasm. I've said it a hundred times, that's why you don't get anywhere with women either. You want to emphasize your strong points instead of fretting about your weaknesses. And you want to keep well away from anything in the least like humour – it's simply not your bag. No one can do anything about that. Now I, for instance, don't know the first thing about soufflés.'

I looked out of the window at the Eiffel Tower again. Surely the Fête Arc-en-Ciel should be starting soon. Loud music, the rainbow, a boisterous atmosphere all over the city – those, I thought, would be suitable reasons for ending our meeting. There wasn't much to discuss on my side anyway. And then basically the meeting would have passed off very well. Because although Chen had staged his usual show, the blow below the belt I'd feared over Leon's arrest hadn't come. Perhaps he simply hadn't clicked on my list of candidates for examination plus descriptions of their cases over the last few days. It wouldn't have been so surprising; after all, there'd been nothing on my list for weeks on end. So perhaps he didn't even know about Leon's arrest.

I really must make sure I uncover something genuinely important some time soon, I thought, and then everyone else, more particularly Chen, could get lost!

'Hey, Max, don't look so fierce. It was only a joke. Ha, ha, ha. Get the idea?'

'Okay, Chen.' I sat up straight and pulled a pen and paper towards me. My sign that I wanted to get down to business at last. And then I mentioned the only thing I knew worth mentioning. 'I suppose you've been informed about the building in the Rue de la Roquette, next to that Saffron Shop?'

'The Saffron Shop,' he repeated slowly. 'No, I haven't. Why should I, and who'd have informed me?'

'It seems there are illegals living there.'

'Aha.' He began picking his teeth with his fingers. 'Who says so?'

'Task-Force Safeguarding Peace. They've arrested an Iranian at the Fence who had a note with that address on it. They've been watching the house ever since. Funny they didn't tell you anything. But they probably think it all falls into my half of the area.'

In many places, the line between my area of operations and Chen's ran right through buildings. But instead of keeping double watch on these borderline buildings, I for one hardly bothered about them. Unconsciously, I was probably deliberately leaving them to Chen.

'That's against all the rules.' He pulled a dark strand of something out of his mouth. 'Suppose we were keeping watch on the place too, with a ploy of our own up our sleeve?'

'Well, they've told us about it now.'

'Not me.'

'All right, I've told you now, I can't do more than that. Anyway, I check the building and that whole block regularly, but all the same I never noticed anything. So far as that goes, then, I'm actually grateful to the task force.'

'Hmhm.'

Chen looked at the strand of whatever it was he'd removed from his mouth, flicked it out of the window and went on picking his teeth. He didn't look pleased. Did he by any chance feel he'd been passed over? Instead of informing Super-Chen they'd turned to unimportant Max Schwarzwald? Or had he in fact thought up a ploy, as he put it, and he was afraid our colleagues from the Safeguarding Peace outfit might muck it up for him? But what kind of a ploy, and why hadn't he told me about it? After all, we were both responsible for the building. Did he want to claim any success for himself alone? And did he think he needed more arrests to his credit? Because this morning, of course, *I* had clicked on *his* last week's list of candidates for investigation plus accounts of their cases. I wanted to know how his self-confidence was doing. After all, even Super-Chen must feel he was under pressure after a time when he didn't have too many results that really counted. And what had counted for him last month? A backyard workshop manufacturing simultaneous translation buttons for several banned African languages, a cosmetic surgeon who'd planned to kidnap a girl from the neigh-bourhood, give her the face of a famous Chinese actress, and keep her as a slave in his basement – the cell in the basement had already been equipped with costumes and screenplays – a woman trying to give her seventy-four-year-old husband a heart attack by strapping him into the sexomat suit whenever he was drunk and making him have sex for hours on end, and finally an ordinary burglar who had kept watch on a lawyer's city villa for several days.

Of course Chen was more successful than I was, but when you compared that list with his reputation, the month of May left a lot to be desired. I remembered times when he was bringing two cases before the Examining Committee almost daily.

Anyway, whatever the reason for it, I could tell from his expression that something had soured his mood. Against my will – because I had told myself to keep any emotions out of this – I felt a certain glee, and considering all I'd had to put up with in the last fifteen minutes even a kind of elation. That must have been why now, of all times, I tried a joke.

I cleared my throat and grinned in a way intended to make it clear that I was being ironic.

'Or perhaps *you* smuggled the people in there? Poor, starving illegals, just to help you get a realistic picture of the arguments of international terrorism, so to speak?'

He didn't react, just kept picking about inside his mouth fretfully.

My grin began to feel forced. Why didn't he look at me? I hoped he didn't think I meant it seriously. Nothing was further from my mind than to provoke Chen now, when I hoped we were both almost on the point of leaving. Probably what he'd said this afternoon about my sense of humour – not that it was the first time he'd said such a thing, but in the past I'd always been able to put it out of my mind at once – well, that had probably hurt me more than I'd been willing to admit at first. That was the only way to explain why I'd ventured on to such thin ice as the result of a brief whim. As if I'd said, 'Hey, see what cutting things I can say after all!' And, probably, in the back of my mind: 'All you good looking single women out there, don't think there's no fun with Max Schwarzwald!' Because of course the really annoying part of it was Chen's routine linking of his disparagement to my success with the opposite sex, which certainly was nothing much to speak of at the moment.

Anyway, I was now hoping that he'd been fully occupied with his teeth, hadn't heard what I said, and we could simply go on with our discussion.

Sure enough, the first remark he made, which probably also explained his facial expression, was, 'My teeth are like a network of caves. I always have provisions for two days left in them every time I eat a meal.'

I breathed a sigh of relief. My joke seemed to have sunk like a stone, unnoticed. To make sure it didn't come up again I quickly picked up on what Chen had said and recommended him my dentist, as I had so often done before. Because Chen's trouble with his teeth was nothing new, and I used every opportunity to recommend her anyway, a simple and yet often long-term way of showing sympathy. By now the name of Dr Williams probably sounded like a corny old pun to Chen. It was still a mystery to me why such an ice-cold character was as scared as a small child of going to the dentist. Even though these days there were anaesthetics that meant you really didn't feel anything at all. But the sweat could literally stand out on Chen's brow at the mere mention of the dentist's chair.

So I smiled and was about to say, for the umpteenth time, 'So here we are talking about my wonderful Dr Williams again. If you were just to call her some time ...' And so on.

At that very minute, instead, Chen turned, looked at me as if I were something the dog had thrown up, and said, 'Yes, I do know about the illegals there, and I'm watching them to find whoever smuggled them in. In case you've forgotten, that kind of thing is part of our job. But you only ever pick up on anyone if they hang silly posters on the wall in front of your nose or announce plans for some kind of cigarette deal in your restaurant.'

My unconscious mind had probably been on watch for any mention of Leon all the time, because I replied at once, 'It wasn't just about cigarettes!'

And now came that blow below the belt after all. Perhaps Chen had just been waiting for the right moment.

'Okay, so your friend was big in the drugs trade too. I've heard he was an unsuccessful painter of kitschy pictures who was looking to earn something on the side. But you'd know better, of course, and the way our colleagues tell it makes no sense. Well, I mean ...' Here he cast me a brief, expressionless, but somehow weary glance. 'I mean, who would shop a friend because of a little cigarette dealing? And you don't have that many friends. Be that as it may, maybe your recent results as an Ashcroft agent do not matter to you much, and so far as I'm concerned you can loaf around all you like, but when some jerks from another department start getting active in ours, and I hear about it only when we have our weekly meeting, and then only because you don't have anything else to your credit – well, we'll soon be reaching the point where *I* go to Youssef for a change and tell him about *your* working morale, and how it's a hindrance to me in my job.'

I stared at him. That wasn't just a blow below the belt, it was as if he'd slapped me in the face and then pulled a gun on me. Chen, of all people, threatening to grass on me to Commander Youssef!

Only at a great distance did the question of why this stupid observation bothered him so much emerge in my mind.

'I want to be informed about that kind of thing right away – is that clear?'

'Perfectly clear,' I replied. He was speaking to me the way I spoke to my kitchen staff.

And then, at last, the Veterans' Band began to play. The tune of 'Somewhere Over the Rainbow' came in through the window, and at the same time coloured arch after coloured arch of the rainbow appeared in the sky. Seen from where I was sitting, it was soon arching in all its many colours over both the Eiffel Tower and Chen's head. It looked great.

'Look.' I pointed to the window.

Chen turned, and even that monster had to smile and couldn't take his eyes off it for a while. But I stared at his smooth black hair, the hair that clogged up the sink all the time, and to my slight alarm found that I was imagining splitting his skull with an axe.

Chapter 3

An hour later, I was sitting on the terrace of a brasserie near the Eiffel Tower, drinking my fourth Brooklyn Organic – a New York beer now quite widely distributed in Europe, not least because of state subsidies. Another aspect of the effort not to let the population here forget our North American friends entirely. I was vaguely aware of groups passing along the streets around me, singing, celebrating and waving rainbow-coloured flags, while in the background the Veterans' Band had gone back to playing jazz classics after the much-applauded air ballet, and with every new round of drinks, glasses were raised again at the tables near me in toasts to the rainbow, half of which was now hanging in the sky above the buildings and our heads as if firmly screwed to it.

After that clash with Chen, I'd really meant to drink just one or two beers to calm my nerves before I went to work. But then the questions relating to Chen's bad mood, and my doubts of his rather too smooth explanation that he was observing the illegals to get at the people-smugglers, became more and more pressing and important in my mind, and I had called the head waiter at Chez Max and told him I'd be later than usual today.

I reminded myself of what Chen had said: 'But that's against all the rules,' and 'Suppose we were keeping watch on the place too, with a ploy of our own up our sleeve?' My vague idea that I'd wrong-footed him somehow was getting stronger. Since when did it bother Chen that something was against all the rules? Or why would he describe a state of affairs only hypothetically in the first instance when he planned to present it later as fact? If he really was watching the building, then why, when I said with the best of intentions but untruthfully, hoping to pacify him, 'Anyway, I check the building and that whole block regularly,' why hadn't he reacted in line with his character and his usual mode of conduct? Then he'd have said, 'You check the building regularly? Well, that's the first I've heard of it!' Instead there'd been that long period of picking his teeth, apparently absent-mindedly, and then suddenly he went on the attack: 'Yes, I do know about the illegals there, and I'm watching them to find whoever smuggled them in. In case you've forgotten, that kind of thing is part of our job.' Didn't that look as if he were in a jam, and the only way to change the subject he could think of was to insult me, finally even threaten me? But what kind of a jam? Or rather: how big a jam was it? Because one thing was clear: Chen had wanted to keep the illegals secret from me. That undoubtedly counted as a crime, if not necessarily a serious one. In addition, I'd suspected for a long time that now and then Chen let some poor sod or other get away with something. He simply brought too few of them before the Examining Committee. And to be honest, I even chalked that generosity up to his credit.

But now an entirely different and incomparably graver suspicion reared its head: was it possible that Chen had been fooling me and the entire Ashcroft department for years? Was this perhaps something like the case of the Malmö diamond dealer? The instructor running an advanced training course for Ashcroft agents had cited that case to us, years ago, as an example of a special kind of criminal camouflage. The context had been the Wars of Liberation of 2030, and today of course the story could never have happened so far as the actual circumstances went. Technology for the identification and classification of objects by means of three-dimensional registration is far too advanced for that. But nothing could ever be done, however great the technological innovations, about the spirit animating the diamond dealer's actions. And if my suspicion was confirmed, I saw that spirit and no other in the behaviour of my Ashcroft partner.

For a while during the Wars of Liberation, on account of worldwide economic insecurity, diamonds, along with gold and platinum, were among the only really reliable means of payment, just as they had been in the Middle Ages. It very soon became one of the most pressing tasks of the Euro-Chinese Confederation to get control of, not just the various remaining oilfields around the world, but also all the diamond mines, and defend them. For that reason, the Resource Islands Department, a part of the Ministry of Economic Affairs and responsible for ensuring supplies of raw materials to the Western and Asian world – the 'islands' themselves, of course, being surrounded not just by water but by Second World nations usually hostile to us – well, the Resource Islands Department then employed hundreds of building contractors, including Björn Hallsund of Malmö. Many of the diamond mines and diamond-cutting works that had come under Euro-Chinese administration needed new buildings, since they had often been cut off from the surrounding country overnight in the course of the fighting and now required villas for the business managers, terraced houses for the workers and administrative staff, barracks for the military, easily isolated accommodation for communities of local workers and other employees, as well as swimming pools, tennis courts, canteens, an airport that could be used for military purposes, streets, bridges and so on. Hallsund and his wife regularly flew between building sites in the Congo and his native Sweden, and the local police (there were no Ashcroft offices yet at the time) soon began to suspect that Hallsund was smuggling diamonds on his weekly flights. He and his wife were observed by the police visiting illegal Stockholm bureaux de change where diamonds were exchanged for gold or euros. Furthermore, Hallsund also met receivers and diamond dealers known in the city, and bought apartment block after apartment block in Sweden and Denmark, transactions which he could never have afforded on his officially declared income.

But in spite of the early initial suspicion, and a whole series of clues backing it up, it was over a year before the investigators worked out how the Hallsunds were getting the diamonds past airport security, and then they were finally caught in the act. Their trick was so simple and obvious that one of the investigators described it in an article entitled 'Losing the Glasses on Your Nose', written for a specialist criminological magazine, and commented: 'When I think of the case, I still shake my head even years later, feeling bewildered and slightly ashamed.'

It went like this: when Hallsund and his flamboyant wife Inga, who was always showily dressed even in everyday life, left Sweden to fly to the Congolese mines, Inga wore necklaces, rings, bracelets, sometimes even a tiara, as if they were flying not to a remote mine but to some sultan's wedding. However, as Inga hardly ever appeared in public anyway without being decked out like some kind of Christmas tree worth millions, the investigators thought of it only at the start. Her jewellery was inspected and registered twice, on leaving the country and on coming in again, and neither time could anything be found wrong: Inga came back with the same stones and necklaces as she had worn when she flew out. In addition, at the second check on her jewellery the couple began acting to the officials searching them and their baggage with such maliciously sarcastic condescension, virtually mounting a savage attack on them, that the security officers on all the day and night shifts were soon glad to give up checking the two of them too thoroughly. At the airport, Hallsund would often address them, even from a distance, with remarks such as, 'Well, dirty pigs, want to get your sweaty hands on my wife's underwear again? Diamonds? You must be joking! You probably don't get too many dates, not on your salaries, so you have to do a bit of groping and pawing at work – gives you something to fantasize about later, right? And you let the gay ones loose on me! Last week one of them was stroking me right down there when he did the body search – is that why you join the border security troops, to get those opportunities?'

(Such, anyway, were his words as reported by the lecturer taking our training course, who had enjoyed recounting the story in detail, and but for whose dramatic presentation the parallel with Chen's behaviour wouldn't have been very likely to occur to me.)

In addition, the fuss he made always attracted a crowd of passengers and airport employees, and the security officer not only had to put up with insults and obscenities but also the attention of members of the public, watching with expressions ranging from sympathy to amusement. And the more members of the public there were, the more Hallsund stepped up the pace. In the process, of course he never forgot to mention that he had governmental backing.

'… Would you dirty pigs like to know who's having to keep dinner waiting for me while you fumble us?'

'Mr Hallsund, we're only doing our job.'

'Ah, well, I'll tell that to the Minister for Economic Affairs: the dirty pigs are only doing their job, and their job is feeling up my lovely Inga's breasts and between her legs. The Minister won't like it. Because shall I tell you why he invites me so often? For Inga's sake, of course. He'd like to feel her up himself, but seeing that he's not a border security officer but only Minister for Economic Affairs, he …'

'Would you open your bag, please, Mr Hallsund?'

'By all means. Look, chock-full of diamonds − smelly sock diamonds, sweaty T-shirt diamonds, the famous and unique aftershave diamond … Anyway, all the Minister for Economic Affairs can do with my Inga is stare at her neckline like an idiot the whole time. He's kind of in love all the same, and jealous, and what he *can* do, on account of his position, is to get certain persons − his rivals of a sort - fired from airport security and customs …'

'What's in this package, Mr Hallsund?'

'Oh God, now you've caught me after all! A whole box full of diamond chocolates! Oh no, oh no, oh no, oh my God!'

'Can't you keep your silly gob shut for half a minute?'

'Help! Police! I'm laying big juicy charges, I've been insulted! Keep my silly gob shut! Is that any way to speak to a man travelling on government business? May I see your name badge, please? You over there, ladies and gentlemen, you're my witnesses ...'

Meanwhile Inga Hallsund didn't say a word, but stretched lasciviously on tables and chairs, touching herself and the security officers sensually during the search, sometimes with deliberate provocation, sometimes apparently unintentionally, moaning and squealing, running her tongue over her lips, putting pens, plastic water bottles or anything else that came to hand in her mouth, and playing her part in what the airport staff were soon calling the Inga and Björn Show. A good many of them arranged to take a break on Friday evenings when the flight from Barcelona arrived so as to be near the security area, in the hope of seeing a new turn added to the show.

You also had to know that at the time Barcelona was the major transit airport for flights from the Greater South, Far South and Farther South regions newly created after the Wars of Liberation, comprising all of what had previously been Africa. Flights from those regions landed in Barcelona without mention of any place of departure, only a numerical code that for the airport staff contained all they needed to know in order to handle the aircraft. Apart from that, it was much the same as with fruit: the airport of a plane's or passenger's departure was always given as the first airport where it landed on Euro-Asian territory. For passengers who lived in Barcelona or simply wanted to stay there after landing, that meant going the long way round through Valencia or Montpellier so that they would have the right to leave Barcelona airport. That was why the Hallsunds officially flew back from Spain every Friday evening, and not even they, with the provocative scenes they staged, would have dreamed of proclaiming to the world that they had been in the Greater Far South region. Although the Civil Code did not yet have the clause about attacks on the Euro-Asian community of values on its statutes, so you couldn't be charged with offences against it, it was already taken for granted in Europe that you didn't mention the world beyond the Fence unless you were willing to run the risk of being lumped in with the likes of terrorists.

The security officers, anyway, soon preferred to wave the Hallsunds through, and even refused to be provoked by Björn Hallsund's challenging references to the jewellery that his wife was still wearing like a proud savage.

'Hey, dirty pigs, take a look at all those kilos of sparkly stuff my Inga is carrying around with her again. The best possible place to hide a few fine stones from Barcelona, wouldn't you say?'

'Please go on through, Mr Hallsund.'

'Or don't you at least want a quick look at Inga's genital piercing? Where's the security dyke to check up on it? Maybe we've fitted a few superb diamonds in those parts too. And look closely – don't you think it's all hanging down a little too heavily there, almost like a cow's udder?'

'Mr Hallsund, you are holding the other passengers up.'

'Oh, come on! I can remember days when we were held up for over an hour, just because the security dyke …'

'Piss off, Hallsund.'

But with time, evidence piled up that diamonds were being smuggled out of the mines that Hallsund visited. More and more frequently, cameras or members of the security service saw workers there in the process of stealing. All the same, the stones were seldom found during the obligatory search when anyone left the diamond-cutting workshops. It was noticeable, however, that between the moment of theft and the time of their body search, the workers always paused briefly somewhere in Hallsund's vicinity as he inspected a wall, a roof, or something of the kind.

So at the airport they began looking closely at the Hallsunds again, although playing it down as far as possible. In that, as it turned out later, they made a bad mistake: they were looking for hiding-places. The more unusual and unimaginable a place seemed to be for hiding diamonds, the more hopefully did the security officers set about examining it. The wheels on suitcases, shoelaces, inside aspirin tablets, Hallsund's dental crowns, match-heads, and all kinds of other things.

Weeks passed in which neither the X-ray devices nor searches of the checked bags produced any result; the Hallsunds were clean. The border security officers, who still kept getting evidence pointing to them from the security services in the mines, began to despair.

Until one day, one of them simply blew his top. Yet again, Hallsund was loudly carrying on about breasts and his government mandate or something, his voice echoing all over the customs area, when the aforesaid officer suddenly went red in the face, started shouting at Hallsund and didn't stop, so that Hallsund's vulgarities and threats were almost drowned out and for the moment he couldn't intimidate anyone. Still bawling them out, the official forced the couple, at pistol-point, to hand over all their jewellery, watches and piercings – Björn Hallsund too would be wearing a ring or a pearl or something of the kind. While Hallsund immediately phoned his lawyer, and the officials were afraid his connections really would lead to governmental powers of some kind showing up and taking the jewellery, the whole case and their own jobs away, a quick examination showed that Inga's necklaces did indeed contain stolen diamonds.

'Another small contribution to the water supply?'

The waiter had stopped at my table with a friendly and rather mischievous smile. Brought abruptly back from my thoughts, I didn't understand what he was saying at first. I looked into his round, benevolent face, and vaguely grasped that in some way or other his question was meant to be a joke. I felt a momentary pang.

It was incredible: not only did I loathe Chen from the bottom of my heart, I had just been weighing up the possibility that he might have been in the service of international terrorism for years, and yet he and his derisive remarks kept getting me down. *You want to keep well away from anything in the least like humour – it's simply not your bag.*

Not for the first time I was judging myself without wanting to – and, if I thought about it for a second, even against my will – by Chen's comments, which were probably just arbitrary and intended to be coarse. Yes, there were situations in which he almost seemed to me to embody some kind of higher authority to which I must answer. That was the only way of explaining why the possibility of my failing to understand the waiter's not particularly cryptic utterance at once almost paralysed me for a moment.

'I was asking whether you'd like another,' said the waiter, ending the short silence, and at the same moment the penny dropped. I quickly interrupted him. 'Yes, please, a double.' I winked at him in a knowing and ironic way to smooth over my brief moment of bafflement.

'On its way,' he replied, took my empty glass and disappeared into the bar.

If you bought a bottle or an 0.5 glass of Brooklyn Original beer, fifteen cents went to support the maintenance of a clean water supply all over the world. It was one of the countless Buy&Help products now available. For instance, if you bought a fermentation-powered SMW (Shanghai Motor Works) car, you were saving half an Asian elephant – which was why those who could afford it would buy two SMWs at once, save a whole elephant and get the right to give it a name, which would be tattooed behind its left ear. Or when you bought a jar of Illy coffee you were donating ten per cent to a medical research project aiming to enable men to get pregnant through uterus implants. In principle, of course, all these were extremely praiseworthy ventures, although it was clear that sales-based calculations were very much to the fore, which was why I took hardly any notice of the Buy&Help campaigns. At least, I was not always automatically aware that the consumption of Brooklyn Organic helped to maintain the water supplies of the world. And at Chez Max, I reflected, we served Jever beer instead.

The waiter soon came back with an 0.5 tankard, put it down in front of me and said, 'Cheers.'

Although I already had four small beers inside me, I drained half the tankard in a single draft. I needed to feel slightly tipsy, or I couldn't bear the suspicion that Chen's more or less banned political propaganda and pseudo-moralizing digressions could also have been just a trick. Could he really have been deliberately expressing himself so frankly and outrageously all this time to keep people from thinking he was doing anything but indulging a taste for sour jokes? Had I been falling for a latter-day Hallsund over the last four years? And above all: would I be able to unmask Super-Chen, the pride of Ashcroft Central Office, Paris, as a criminal enemy of the state?

'Hey, dirty pigs, take a look at all those kilos of sparkly stuff my Inga is carrying around with her again.' Surely that, quite apart from a similar association between humans and animals, was in principle much the same as saying, 'People are swine, it's always been like that, it always will be, and the world they create is a pig of a world.' At least it was if you were in the service of international terrorism, the sole aim of which was the destruction of our Western 'pig of a world' - the very same words used by many of its supporters.

And what was the first step, what had been the foundations of almost all attacks carried out on Euro-Asian territory since the Fence went up? Getting their people in. Wretched desperados, ready for anything, to be accommodated in hiding for a while, for instance in an ordinary-looking building in the Rue de la Roquette, before they blew themselves sky-high at a popular festival or in a place as internationally well known as possible. Or as Chen had put it a little while ago, when I couldn't have guessed what an ambiguous meaning it might have for him: 'Once it was said that half of humanity lived below the poverty line; today it's said that half of humanity are potential terrorists.'

Even here among us, of course, there were people frustrated by the world in general who let themselves be recruited by religious fanatics or preachers of revolution. But experience showed that for the really lethal attacks – such as the blowing up of Cologne Cathedral with over a thousand dead, or the chemical bombing of the Belgrade Love Parade, death toll over two thousand – the hope-lessness, ignorance and hatred of a few young men fresh from some Second World slum were needed. For even the most fervent Euro-Asian sympathizer with so-called freedom movements was probably glad, in some hidden corner of his heart, that over thirty years ago his parents or grandparents had either managed or opted to stay this side of the Fence. For instance, if he could sit quietly here on the terrace of this brasserie while he sympathized, drinking a beer or something else, enjoying the sight of the new rainbow, or maybe for all I know deploring the decadence of such an expensive and useless invention – well, at least he didn't have to fear being shot by the soldiers of some dictator or religious leader for his pro-opposition views, as they did in the Far South or Southeast. Apart from the fact that most of the potential assassins born in the Confederation were of course rendered harmless by Ashcroft agents before they committed any terrorist offences.

I drank some of my beer and looked at the time. Lieutenant Gilbert, our colleague from the Task-Force Safeguarding Peace responsible for surveillance of the building in the Rue de la Roquette, had promised to call me back over half an hour ago. Almost everything depended on why Chen had not been told about the surveillance.

And suppose it had just been an oversight? What if, for instance, Gilbert said, 'Oh yes, our mistake. If we'd known you divide the buildings on the borderline half and half between you, of course we'd have informed Monsieur Chen too. Why on earth wouldn't we? Several of my people would have been glad to exchange a few words with the famous Chen of the Ashcroft Agency. What did you say your name was again?'

I emptied my glass and signalled to the waiter to bring me another large beer.

… Well then, I was just unlucky.

★

'Max Schwarzwald?'

'Speaking.'

'Lieutenant Gilbert here. Sorry, our meeting took a little longer than expected. You wanted some information about our operation in your area?'

'Well … it's about my partner Chen Wu.'

'Hmhm.'

'You know, the famous Chen of the Ashcroft Agency.'

'Of course.'

'Yes, well … I hope I'm not interfering with anything …'

'Oh, come on, Monsieur Schwarzwald, we're all pulling together.'

He was right there, of course, but the Task-Force Safeguarding Peace, answering directly to the Ministry of Defence, ranked much higher in the pecking order – or should I say pulling order? – than most of the other Eurosecurity departments. Since TFSP was internationally active, and besides safeguarding the Fence was really responsible for everything in the nature of illegal trafficking between the First and Second Worlds, it was regarded as a kind of James Bond unit. Its members were always on call to go anywhere around the globe, risking their lives on daring missions and snapping up the really tough nuts from Cape Town to Vladivostok. That was why what TFSP said traditionally carried a little more weight than anything similar coming from other departments. For instance, the Three Element Fighter had been developed mainly in response to pressure from the top brass of TFSP. They had been complaining for years that their security people on the sixty-thousand-kilometres-long border were occupied more with the coordinated deployment of shipping, jeeps and aircraft, and ensuring communication between them all, than with pursuing smugglers and terrorists. In addition – and so far as my business was concerned this was far from being the least of it – it was no secret that TFSP, as a department operating internationally with a world-wide network of informants, always worked closely with Eurosecurity Self-Protection, the department that policed the police forces.

'You told me last week about surveillance of a building in the Rue de la Roquette.'

'Hmhm.'

'I don't know if you're aware that the building lies right on the line between my area and Chen's, and so we are both responsible for monitoring it.'

'We're aware of it now.'

'How do you mean?'

'During our surveillance, we noticed Monsieur Chen obviously going about the same job as us.'

'You mean keeping watch on the building?'

'Which is all to his credit. He clearly gets to know what's going on in his manor.'

Was that meant to needle me personally?

'All the same, you didn't inform him of your people's presence. At least, Wu was very surprised when I told him about it today.'

Lieutenant Gilbert paused for a moment. Then he said, 'We assumed he'd hear about it from you.'

That was odd. You didn't expect TFSP to replace established methods of procedure, where everyone's spheres of competence were respected, by an 'Oh, word will have got around' kind of attitude.

'But it could well have been that, in our sensitive field

of operations, I started by supposing that if Wu wasn't told there must be reasons for it.'

'What sort of reasons?'

'That's what I'm asking you. Your department has a reputation for working very precisely and conscientiously. That doesn't fit the picture of its being left almost to chance whether Wu was told or not.'

Once again he paused before answering. Had I been too forthright? On the other hand, this was my chance. If I could be sure that TFSP had suspicions of Chen, I'd begin shadowing him myself this very evening. First, I had a perfectly good reason if Chen spotted me at it. Second, if there was any possibility of nabbing Chen, then I thought it was mine by right.

'Let me put it this way: we know that on the basis of his success over the years, Monsieur Wu has a certain freedom to operate. Not just in assessing potential or actual crimes, where he may turn a blind eye to minor offences, but also, as you as his partner must know only too well, in his view of the state of affairs in our society. When we had established that the illegals and potential assassins under our own surveillance were also in Monsieur Wu's area, and he knew of their presence, we grasped the opportunity, you might say, and deliberately let things take their course in a way designed to intrigue him. How did he react to discovering that you and not he had been informed by us, then?'

I thought I heard an undertone in his voice saying something like, 'You of all people, not he, the star of the Ashcroft Agency?'

Without stopping to think about it, I said, 'It didn't seem to matter to him.'

'Oh yes?'

'What did you expect?'

'As I was saying, nothing in particular. But of course Monsieur Wu knows that's not the way to follow correct procedure.'

Had I tripped myself up?

'You think he would normally be annoyed?'

'That would at least be an understandable reaction. On the other hand, there may be any number of good reasons why, as you say, it didn't seem to matter to him. The simplest and most likely being that he had spotted my men.'

This time I was the one to pause. Then I explained, in tones of sincere concern, 'Look, Lieutenant Gilbert, I'll be perfectly frank with you. As Wu's partner I certainly don't always have an easy time of it, but we've shared the same area of operations for over four years, and I like to think that despite all the difficulties we've grown into a kind of team. And to be honest, I even admire Wu quite often. I think he could properly be described as a brute but a brainbox – and with him, you don't get one without the other. Anyway, I can hardly imagine working with anyone else. But now you come along, and you indicate that Wu is under observation. Or as you put it, you let things take their course in a way designed to intrigue him. You didn't say how or why, and I'm the one who feels most intrigued by that. *I* have to work with Wu, I have to be able to trust him, I can't keep asking myself the whole time what it means if he isn't annoyed, or perhaps he is annoyed, or whatever. So if there is any suspicion that he is involved in anything outside the usual legal framework, I think it's your duty to tell me about it.'

I stopped and thought of Chen's homely truism, often repeated: 'If someone begins by saying, "I'll be perfectly frank with you", you can forget about it.'

Lieutenant Gilbert cleared his throat, and then said, with slight hesitation, 'But there's nothing for me to tell you about. Even if we – or I should say the Self-Protection department – wouldn't mind doing so if there was. We in TFSP got dragged into this only because of that guy at the border.'

'You mean the Self-Protection people would like to have something against Wu?'

'Well, you know how it goes: someone talks big, thinks he's a big noise, you feel like shaking him and saying: stop that, behave yourself. But if there's no way you can do him any harm, it's just so much hot air.'

'Since when did Self-Protection have no way of doing someone from Eurosecurity any harm?'

'He's not just anyone from Eurosecurity. If word got round that relatively unfounded disciplinary measures had been taken against Chen Wu – well, it wouldn't have a wonderful effect on the climate of our working environment.'

'How do you mean, unfounded? Don't take this the wrong way, but we both know that Self-Protection, in the fight against corruption and counter-democratic activities, is constantly being obliged not just to find grounds for something but, let's say, to leave such grounds lying around the place themselves.'

'Yes, that can happen. But I'm assuming that such actions are taken more carefully in Chen Wu's case. He can't be expected to crumple in the face of an accusation that makes no sense.'

It took me a moment to digest his assessment. Although I was sure that within Eurosecurity I knew Chen better than anyone else, and I'd had only too much first-hand experience of his aura and his effect on others, it still surprised me to find what a reputation he clearly had in all departments. In any case, it was extraordinary to find that Self-Protection had inhibitions about palming any clever little tricks off on him. On the other hand, the officers responsible were presumably right: accusing him of taking drugs or putting an underage girl in his bedroom wouldn't discipline him. Far from it: I could see him in my mind's eye drumming up all our colleagues at Ashcroft Central Office, making a big speech in the conference hall and describing, with relish and in every alleged or actual detail, how a few small, frustrated, jealous 'sodding colleagues' of ours from Self-Protection were trying to pin something on a successful man just because they had nothing better to do, and they wanted to demonstrate their power. Of course he wouldn't be the only person present to have had trouble with Self-Protection one way or another, and I could already hear the shouts of applause and people calling, 'You show 'em, Chen!' and, 'Fuck Self-Protection.'

'I understand,' I said at last. 'Well, I know where things are then.'

'I'm sorry, Monsieur Schwarzwald, I do see that the situation's not entirely straightforward for you. I suggest you go on working with Wu as usual, and for the rest let things take their course.'

'There's nothing else I *can* do. But I do very much hope that Self-Protection will come to understand that Chen Wu is a special – and above all an especially successful – colleague, so he must be allowed a few quirky little opinions of his own.'

'I'm afraid I can't go along with you there. Only recently, Wu said in public to one of our commanders that we were using firing squads along the Fence – which God knows can't be dismissed as a quirky little opinion.'

'I know, it was in our cafeteria, I was there. Of course, that was monstrous. I can only say, in his defence, that at least he doesn't spread such horror stories in secret. This way it can be discussed – as in fact in that case it was – and such ridiculous claims can be refuted.'

It was becoming clearer to me all the time that Chen was taking the Hallsund line.

'Hmhm, if that's how you see it. All the same, I don't think the right to free speech means anyone can talk any dangerous nonsense that occurs to him. But of course I understand that you want to protect your partner.'

'Thanks, Lieutenant. Then might I ask you a favour?'

'Go ahead.'

' If there should be anything backing up the – well, let's say the wish of Self-Protection for Wu to be up to no good of some kind with the illegals in the Rue de la Roquette, would you please let me know as soon as possible?'

'Of course. But as I said, I think Wu is simply doing his job.'

'Let's hope so,' I said. Then we finished the call. I switched off my mobile and took a large draught of the fresh beer that the waiter had now brought me.

I ask you – 'simply doing his job'! Chen Hallsund was twice as clever as Self-Protection or TFSP, that was all. *I* had seen his fury when he learned about the TFSP surveillance, and no one was going to tell me that he had acted that way because, in Lieutenant Gilbert's words, correct procedure hadn't been followed. Correct proce-dure! The mere phrase usually had Chen in fits of nasty laughter. For him only idiots spoke that way, trying to compensate for something or other with haughty remarks.

No, Chen's fury had arisen from his sense of an immediate threat. For a moment, a crack had appeared in his Hallsund façade, and I was going to make sure the whole thing came tumbling down.

Chapter 4

I had no real plan. I simply wanted to stick to Chen like glue and stay stuck until he led me to the 'diamonds'.

I was in no doubt now that he was involved in something criminal. The only question was, how far in was he? Did he belong directly to some terrorist outfit? Was he perhaps one of its leaders – in line with his intelligence and abilities – and responsible for the planning and organisation of assassinations in the Greater Paris area? Or was he solely active as an informant and in rendering assistance? Naturally, working as an Ashcroft agent would give him great opportunities for that. What he could discover from the Eurosecurity computer alone about planned raids by the security services and investigations in progress in France would be enough to thwart much of what was described as *the offensive against international terrorism carried out at all times and in all places.*

I remembered the leader of one police unit complaining of an incident in the Ashcroft canteen only last week: he and his team had planned a second raid on some suspect apartments, and once again found them empty in a way suggesting that the people he was after had been warned only just before they went in. One of the apartments had been in the district next to Chen's area of operations. That didn't necessarily mean anything, but it fitted the picture. What was more, I knew that in his official capacity as a municipal gardener Chen helped his colleagues in the neighbouring district out now and then, when there was some large landscaping job to be done.

Or perhaps the terrorists were simply making use of Chen. In the naïve belief that he was helping so-called 'poor refugees' – itself well known to be a contradiction in terms since, after all, the poor couldn't afford the trip to Europe – he was finding them accommodation, perhaps getting hold of forged papers, and passing on secret information to people who had managed to persuade him that they were acting in the true service of humanism. We all knew the way they talked.

However, I found it difficult to link the term 'naïve belief' with Chen's name in the same sentence. It was very much more likely to imagine him using some kind of clever, cynical pseudo-morality to justify the so-called 'Second World struggle for freedom'. Even if, as in the case of the illegals in the Rue de la Roquette and according to Lieutenant Gilbert, we were dealing with Iranians. As for their 'struggle for freedom', I had only recently watched an almost unbearable report on film from SII, the Secret International Information Service of Eurosecurity. For decades, the regime in former Iran had been dominated by a kind of ultra-religious murderous frenzy, its twin pillars being hatred of the Western world and constant prayer, not to mention the persecution of any dissidents. The film showed an entire family, from grandfather to grandson, being beheaded because the father had hidden one of his sons, a boy of ten, to keep him from going to a training camp for suicide bombers. You saw executioners with enormous swords on a wooden platform, thousands of eager spectators standing around, a cleric chanting prayers, and a young man holding up the severed heads in front of the faces of those family members who were still alive. Even the James Bonds of TFSP avoided venturing into the Greater Persia area as much as possible.

So much for the 'struggle for freedom'. But also so much for the likelihood that an illegal Iranian immigrant was anything other than a trained assassin. How many normal, peace-loving people could there still be in such a society? And how many of those could successfully get past a dense network of police, secret services, 'guardians of religion' and informers, and leave the country? And then they would have to get over our Fence! By that point at the latest, the chances were nil. Passing the Fence, one might say, was possible only with logistical and technical instructions and the help of the Iranian police apparatus.

And was Chen supposed to have no idea of all that?

But whatever criminal level he was operating on, I'd have to actually find him before I could catch him.

After my phone conversation with Lieutenant Gilbert, I had walked round to the eleventh arrondissement, and I had now been standing for the last half hour outside the building at number 121 Rue de la Roquette. On the third floor, where the illegals were living, lights were switched on, and looking through the kitchen window I could see a woman going back and forth. Presumably she was preparing supper. Well, even assassins have to eat.

There were curtains over the other windows, and now and then I saw shadowy forms moving behind them.

Obviously our conversation at the office had not made Chen decide to take immediate steps. On the other hand, it couldn't be so easy to find somewhere else to take the illegals in a hurry, and very likely there were explosives and weapons to be organized. After all, you couldn't just carry bundles of such things through the city. And then, of course, there were the TFSP men. On the whole they weren't fools, you had to trick them.

I had walked up and down the street twice, searching the windows of the building opposite the illegals' apartment for any signs of the surveillance team. A device of some kind placed on the window pane to hide a camera; suspiciously dimly lit rooms; or simply someone half-hidden behind a curtain looking across the street. But they could have preferred to plant bugs on the floors above or below the illegals.

It was nothing out of the ordinary for Eurosecurity departments to take a place over for a short time. Usually the public health authority was sent ahead, citing the risk of termite or fungal infestation on the building structure as the reason why interior and exterior walls, and any exposed beams in the apartment, had to be investigated and observed around the clock for a certain period of time.

I looked at the time. It was nearly eight-thirty. Around me, the first shops were closing for the night, the aperitif bars were beginning to empty and the restaurants were filling up.

I thought for a moment of Chez Max and wondered whether to call again and say I probably wouldn't be in at all this evening. But then I decided that my absence wasn't going to be any particular surprise to my staff, most of whom had been there for years. After all, not so long ago I had often been away from the place all evening. But a point came when I was tired of inventing new Mireilles and Ninas in the interests of my Ashcroft investigations, and meeting my employees' risqué queries and comments with the same meaningful smile. Especially at times when the only Mireilles and Ninas with whom I had any contact – well, contact of a kind – were those I'd stored in the sexomat. Quite possibly that was even the main reason for the neglect of my Ashcroft work. It had been so undignified to be teased all day about some romance or other, and then at night – often after hours spent alone in the windy entrance to some building – to climb into the sexomat suit behind carefully drawn curtains. So I had begun to cross the occasional suspect off my list, then all cases in which the likelihood of success seemed slight, and so on, until criminals actually had to drop from the sky in front of my feet before I would pay them any attention.

And on this mild spring evening it wasn't likely I'd be spared one of the head waiter's little quips, such as 'Ah, the merry month of May, Max our boss wants a good lay'.

So instead of listening to silly jokes, I tapped the number of the Ashcroft Agency Localization Office into my mobile. Every Ashcroft agent had a tiny transmitter through which he could be located precisely by satellite anywhere in Europe, to the square metre. If you didn't have the transmitter with you and were caught without it, you needed very good reasons to escape disciplinary measures. Officially the system was 'for urgent cases', but first and foremost, of course, it was for checking up on us. No wonder that the idea came from Self-Protection.

A woman's voice answered the phone. 'Ashcroft Localization Office, my name is Bonnet, may I ask you for voice identification, please?'

I recited the password employed for the purpose, quoting the wording of the Treaty of Europe: 'Liberté, égalité, sécurité.'

A few seconds later the woman replied, 'Good evening, Monsieur Schwarzwald. What can I do for you?'

'Good evening. I'm looking for my partner Chen Wu, eleventh arrondissement.'

'Would you tell me your reasons, please?'

'It's about a group of illegals living in a building in our area of operations. We're after the people-smugglers who got them in, and just now it looks as if the illegals are about to leave the house. I need Wu to help me keep them under surveillance.'

'Why don't you call him?'

'I've tried, but he must have switched his telephone off. I only wanted to know if he's anywhere near just now. Then I could get hold of him in a hurry.'

I very much hoped the woman wasn't too quick on the uptake and wouldn't ask for Chen's number, so that she could check what I said. Getting information out of the Localization Office was always a dodgy business. If it wasn't a genuine emergency, they were quick to suspect you of trying on something a little crooked with whoever you were looking for. It was a fact that agents quite often tried cornering annoying colleagues that way, or even ruining their lives by surprising them in delicate situations. Generally there was sex of some kind involved.

'I should tell you that I'm putting your reasons on record.'

'Of course.'

I didn't suppose that Chen would be applying to see the localization records over the next few days. And after that he wouldn't be able to apply to do anything any more.

'One moment, please … Monsieur Wu is at present in a small park on the Boulevard Richard Lenoir, corner of the Rue Pelée.'

I thanked her and set out.

★

Normally it wouldn't have surprised me to see Chen still gardening at nine in the evening or even later. Everyone knew, and it always caused our colleagues to shake their heads, between amusement and surprise, that Chen gardened with as much commitment and devotion as if plants were considerably closer and more valuable to him than human beings. I had actually seen him talking to a broom bush. Apart from that – say what you like about him, and offhand as his behaviour could be – Chen was extremely disciplined and conscious of his duty. If he had made up his mind in the morning to lay out a flower bed or prune trees before supper but got around to it rather late because of the Fête Arc-en-Ciel or something of that kind, he would put off eating until midnight if necessary.

But when I went down the Boulevard Richard Lenoir and saw Chen in the park mentioned by Madame Bonnet, on his knees among a number of wooden pots containing rose bushes, digging holes by the light of the street lamps and filling them with water from a hose, I was absolutely baffled for a moment.

He couldn't be serious! Did he really have nothing better to do this evening? I almost had to prevent myself from obeying my first impulse and simply going over to bawl him out, ask if he still had all his marbles? The illegals, the TFSP team, our argument that afternoon – did he really not care a fuck, as he would put it, about any of that?

I stopped short, and after a moment I walked on with my face averted. A young woman was sitting on a bench near Chen. Out of the corner of my eye I could see that he was talking to her as he took a rose bush and placed it carefully in one of the holes.

Fifty metres away there were bright neon lights; an ad

for sparkling water and the name of a café. The café was right opposite the park, and I hoped I could keep watch on Chen and the woman through its window.

When I went in I was met by the smell of stale beer and washing-up water. The café was empty except for the owner. He was washing glasses. I sat down at the bar, ordered an espresso, and turned to the window. Chen and the woman were about seventy metres away. When I put my special binocular-lensed glasses on, I might have been right there with them.

Chen was just saying something, glancing over his shoulder as he spoke, and the woman laughed. Looking through the binocular glasses, I could see she was attractive. She must have been about ten years younger than Chen, with a pretty, round, cheerful face, and she was wearing a close-fitting red suit with a glittering cape and a velvet band in her hair, all very fashionable at the time. It looked as if she'd prettied herself up for a dinner date.

A dinner date with Chen? He was wearing grey working clothes, and was spattered with mud.

Although God knows I had other things to think about, I couldn't help reflecting that this wasn't the first time I'd seen Chen with a woman who looked as if she played in a much higher league. As these women were always Europeans, I assumed that his Asian origin gave him the attraction of exoticism. On the other hand, I'd often approached Chinese women who hadn't been tempted to go out with *me* because of my white skin. Perhaps it really was something to do with a sense of humour. I was always reading, in the singles magazines, how important that was to women. *You want to keep well away from anything in the least like humour – it's simply not your bag.*

I turned to the café owner. 'And a double Calvados, please.'

And he kept his pretty companion waiting because he wanted to finish a rose bed that could just as well have been planted tomorrow or next week!

Apart from everything else. For it couldn't be ruled out that this might be his last date for a long time.

Or was that my problem? Was I too keen to impress, did I try too hard with women? I'd read a fair bit about that too.

'Cheers.'

The café owner put my espresso and Calvados down in front of me, casting me an unfriendly glance. Perhaps he'd really wanted to close the place.

I sipped the Calvados and wondered what was going on in Chen's mind at this moment. Nothing at all? All his appointments for the day duly discharged? Discussion at Ashcroft Central Office, then planting flowers and meeting a woman, and the undercover assassins could wait until tomorrow? Work is work and strong liquor is strong liquor?

But how did all that fit the picture of the idealist that he must be, somewhere deep inside him, an idealist who, though in a negative sense, was risking his freedom and possibly his life to change the world? Or was he active as a terrorist in the same cold-blooded way that he worked as an Ashcroft agent? Because for Chen his Ashcroft work seemed to be nothing but an intellectual game. At least, that was roughly what he had said once, when I plucked up my courage after some new tirade of his against the government, the mayor, or something else, and asked him, 'Then why are you still doing this work? I mean, why do you of all people spend so long in the service of our society? You've been an Ashcroft man for over ten years, you could sign your undertaking of silence and retire now, you'd get a good pension and be a free man. You'd have all the time in the world to do nothing but look after your beloved bushes and flowers.'

As so often, he had looked up from a plastic container of Chinese junk food and replied, as if speaking to a rather stupid child, 'Well, sweetie-pie, you ought to have worked that out over the last few years. I like our job. Not all that shit about defending democracy and safeguarding the future, that's your cup of tea. But I like to sit around watching people, trying to make sense of their behaviour, now and then seeing a crime coming in advance. I haven't been among the Ashcroft agents with the best quotas in Paris every year because I have aims and values of some kind, it's because I know my trade. And I know it because I like it.'

If he liked his trade, could he possibly be organizing suicide bombings at the same time? Did he see everything as just a game? Yet he was neither a megalomaniac – at least, not in the sense of being paranoid, really round the bend – nor tired of life. Far from it: he liked eating, even if most of what he ate was revolting, he liked women, loved plants, was a classical music fan, read books, played table tennis, flew to the Highlands of Scotland once a month to go fishing and drink whisky, had a beautiful apartment with a view of the Père Lachaise cemetery, and was a regular visitor – not just because of his Ashcroft work, I felt sure – to the bars and nightclubs of the eleventh arrondissement. Strictly speaking, there wasn't a pleasure in life I'd heard of – or at least something he would consider a pleasure – that he had ever declined. Basically, then, it was a joke that Chen of all people would so often bewail the decadence and craving for pleasure of the Western world, with particular reference to me and my restaurant. It wasn't that he had chosen that oysters, kidneys fried to just the right shade of pink, and a good espresso didn't mean anything to him. And this evening I wasn't even sure about that any more: perhaps it was all part of the great game of Hallsund hide-and-seek that he'd been playing for years. At this point I wouldn't have been totally astonished to hear through the grapevine that, after some successful coup like the death of dozens or sometimes hundreds of white 'oppressors' or the blowing up of the Paris foreign bureau of the Resource Islands Department a few months ago, Chen would go to the Bofinger to celebrate with a contact from the Far Southern or Middle Eastern area, the pair of them scoffing shellfish and drinking Sancerre.

However, even if everything was as it appeared: Chen really didn't appreciate good food himself but on the other hand would fly to Scotland to fish and enjoy rare whiskies, at the same time bad-mouthing his fellow man for thinking no further than the next superficial pleasure – even if the contradiction between his words and his actions couldn't be denied, well, if Chen were asked about it then of course he would come up with some slippery answer. And that was exactly what he'd once given me.

It was one afternoon four years ago, just after we began working as a team: 'What do you mean, how can I reconcile my political stance with a five-room apartment with a roof garden?'

'What can it mean…?' I said. 'How does someone who's always talking about self-indulgence and immorality fix it with his conscience, as a single man and someone working outside the office, to ask the Ashcroft accommodation people for living space enough for a large family in the most densely populated city in Europe with the worst housing shortage per capita?'

'Easy, *mein Führer!* What does it mean? Oh, me stupid primitive slitty-eyes!'

'I didn't mean it like that. Sorry. But the question remains ...'

I was still naïve enough at the time to think that if I could only summon up enough patience and sweet reason, I could get Chen to have a grown-up relationship with mutual respect for each other.

'*Achtung!* The Führer is apologizing!'

'Please, Chen, if I took the wrong tone ...'

'Oh, come off it – the wrong tone! So you think my apartment and what I have to say about human beings contradict each other?'

'No, I just think it's rather striking.'

'Rather striking, well, well!' He gave an affected little cough.

'If you don't like the way I put it, that's no reason to – '

'Then again,' he interrupted me, 'of course it does work the other way around: someone living in a hovel with nothing to eat can't be expected to spare the time to lean back at his ease, thinking about the state the world's in and how to improve it. That would be like saying heart surgery ought to be performed by stroke patients.'

'I don't know what that's got to do with – '

'With my apartment? Simple: a man who lives in an apartment like mine has the chance – and thus the duty – to think about morality more. People like *you* are the contradiction: you earn a pot of money with your restaurant but you still pay only the usual Ashcroft rent for an apartment which isn't exactly tiny itself, you have a holiday home on the Adriatic, you regularly overrun your leave, so I've heard, and with all that relaxed, luxury living, and when you look at the rest of the world you never stop to wonder if everything is really fair and right and proper.'

It was the first time since we'd been put in a team together that Chen had gone beyond the usual grumbling and said something that sounded like propaganda. I was shocked.

As if in a trance, I repeated, 'The rest of the world?' and my heart began to thud at the thought that by *the rest* Chen might mean the part of it that even we were recommended to mention only in certain circumstances. I was already beginning to fear that I'd have to report my new partner to Commander Youssef after only a few weeks of working with him. That wouldn't make a very good impression on our colleagues, however grave my reasons. Team spirit in large quantities was expected in the Ashcroft agency, and rightly so.

Chen smiled as if he were planning to test me with some kind of cunning trap. 'Well, take the Paris suburbs. Ever been there to see how the other half lives, or rather how the vast majority live? Probably not, because what could you talk to them about? They're not all that interested in recipes for ceps.'

Now I knew that Chen had indeed meant the rest of the world on the other side of the Fence. Presumably my sudden uneasiness hadn't escaped him, so he had mentioned the suburbs just to tease me. Or else, he was being a bit more cautious on such subjects at the time.

Later I did visit the suburbs, and if the quality of life couldn't be compared with living in the city centre, there was no real poverty. Far from it: in spite of crowded quarters, food from cheap supermarkets and chains of snack bars, what to me seemed an unusual amount of rubbish in the streets – but that was their own fault, after all – and the ever-present aircraft noise because of the proximity of Subaru Airport, I saw more people publicly laughing, drinking and in lively conversation with each other in that one day than in a whole year in the eleventh arrondissement. That might be because of the hotter, somehow livelier Oriental blood that still unmistakably flowed through the veins of the majority of the people living there, even fifty years or more after the construction of the Fence, which meant without any refreshing of the gene pool. But for me, as I walked around, the noisy, colourful, cheap sparkle of all that hustle and bustle proved one thing above all: however great your outward wretchedness, what counted most in life was your inner attitude. And in purely practical terms, homes in the old quarters of Paris just weren't possible for everyone, even in a society where the government, as our President had once put it, 'guarantees everyone the maximum possible amount of health, comfort and culture.'

But that afternoon four years ago, I hadn't been thinking much about such matters, and I hardly noticed Chen's insulting remark about the ceps recipes. First and foremost, I was relieved that in mentioning the Paris suburbs he'd brought up a subject that could be tackled critically. Hardly a week went by when the media didn't discuss the social ills in the suburbs and their effects: drug crimes, child labour, secret workshops where both legal and illegal immigrants made clothes, where proprietary branded goods were forged, or texts glorifying violence and supporting terrorism were printed. There was prostitution (because of course very few could afford a sexomat), there were gangs of young people, and naturally there were the regular unauthorized demonstrations. In fact the term 'unauthorized demonstrations' was only a synonym for public anti-Israel rallies. It was an open secret in Eurosecurity that, during the Wars of Liberation, the Euro-Asian leadership, by arrangement with the interim US American government, had deliberately left the Israel/Palestine conflict unresolved to provide a safety-valve for their own population if, at a later date, the need to be politically engaged became overwhelming. So it was that at the end of the Wars not only Israel but also the Palestinian territories became part of the Euro-Asian and North American world. To this day, the European government provided both sides with financial and diplomatic support, as well as armaments and secret service information, helping now one and now the other, so that the country – or countries, depending on your political standpoint – was or were never at peace.

So when discontent looked as if it was spreading among the population for some reason or other, for instance a rise in the cost of heating or the taxes on alcohol – and of course that hit the suburbs almost exclusively, because hardly anyone who lived in the city centre would even notice another few cents on a bottle of spirits – when the bars and the places where young people gathered began to seethe with unrest and the Ashcroft agents there gave warning of possible protests against the government, the subject of Israel automatically came up in the news. Ever since the Wars of Liberation a lot of thought had gone into ensuring that nothing in the public mind changed the familiar picture of the mighty Jewish oppressors on one side and the Arab Palestinian freedom fighters on the other. First, anything more complex was of course no use for rousing popular anger and second, in our modern society it was a humiliating but unfortunately undeniable fact that large parts of the population were still not free of prejudice towards our fellow citizens of Jewish descent. Or as an internally circulated Eurosecurity memo said: 'If we cannot entirely root out the evil of anti-Semitism, we will at least exploit it to protect European democracy and thus, necessarily, our Jewish minority.'

The usual method employed by the Mental Health Department, responsible for the protection of democracy and minorities, was to publish the photograph of some 'father', 'brother' or 'son' shot by Israeli soldiers. Or there were films of Israeli soldiers destroying a suicide bomber's family home with diggers in retaliation for their son's action, or cordoning off the borders between Palestinian areas. There was generally a call for demonstrations the next day. That way, people could vent their aggression and anger and forget about price rises or other state demands for the time being. Basically it was a good, sensible arrangement, calling for a very small sacrifice if you thought of the social satisfaction that it provided.

Naturally the media also mentioned attacks by Palestinians and showed pictures of the victims, but who would dare side with the one oppressor we still had in our Western world? Sometimes Jewish student associations organized petitions at the Bastille, or distributed leaflets about the history and mainly peaceful everyday life of Israel. And of course the pamphlets always reminded readers of the Holocaust. But even someone like me, a German who still, after many generations, took on the inherited burden of guilt and was even glad to take it on – after all, it helped me to gain a better understanding of myself and my cultural origins – even those like me had to admit that the subject didn't interest anyone any more, except for jokes about Nazis made in Chen's inimitable style and the annual Never Again Fascism Day.

Condemnation of Israel was the stance to take, as the politically engaged segment of the population had unanimously agreed. Well, no other option was open to them.

They're not all that interested in recipes for ceps ...

What an arrogant idiot! If I'd known then what was clear to me now, I could have replied, 'What, not even your comrades eating their last meal in this world? Or do they have some other term for it before strapping on explosives, going into a department store, preferably picking the children's department, and blowing themselves to bits?'

Because apart from such exceptions as the Rue de la Roquette, most of the potential suicide bombers who had got past the Fence naturally disappeared in the teeming masses of the suburbs.

Or I could have been even wittier, even more cutting; I could have said, 'Oh no? What about recipes for mushroom clouds?'

A terrorist group from the Caucasus really had set off a small, home-made nuclear bomb four years ago in a Moscow suburb. It is true that only a few hundred people had died in the blast, but because the entire contaminated area hadn't been cleared because of the expense, an unofficial report indicated that thousands of its inhabitants died annually from the long-term effects of radiation. To be sure, most of those who had settled in that part of the city since the explosion were Caucasians, 'and that,' said one of our Russian colleagues dryly at the Ashcroft Christmas party, 'has at least brought the whole thing full circle.'

They're not all that interested ... what could someone who so far had seen the suburbs only on the news say in answer to that?

'I think we'd soon find something to talk about,' I said lamely, and then went on the attack myself. 'What were you trying to say anyway? Someone who lives in a hovel can't be expected to think up ways to improve the world, is that it?'

At the time I still assumed that, even for Chen, a *faux pas* – which if interpreted with malicious intent might be a criminal offence – was still a *faux pas*, and what I said would at least shut him up for a moment.

But instead he gave me a bleary stare, then closed his eyes, tilted his head to one side and made snoring noises.

'Oh God!' I exclaimed angrily.

After a while Chen opened his eyes again. 'Max,' he whispered, with a despairing expression on his face, 'dear Max, oh, please don't inform on me for speaking out against the state!'

'Ha, ha,' I said humourlessly.

'Ha, ha!' he imitated me. Then he sat up straight and said, in his normal tone of voice, 'I'm the one who should be informing on you. Mention of improving the world instantly makes *you* think of revolutions or something of the kind. Like a sexually disturbed man who undoes his flies the moment he sees women eating bananas. Let me remind you that it's our task, as the Ashcroft Oath puts it, "to do our daily part towards the constant improvement of the world".'

'But that's not what you meant just now,' I said childishly, and a bit hysterically. As always in an argument with Chen, I was losing my footing. Yet I knew perfectly well that he'd been thinking of anything but the Ashcroft Oath.

'Oh, Max!' Chen cursorily ended the conversation. 'That's no way to have an argument. Sometimes you are just so thick.'

Just so thick! And uttered in such a gentle, warm, totally hopeless tone of voice! Not just that – Chen of all people trying to tell me how to have an argument! So I suppose snoring noises were okay?

I signalled to the café owner to bring me another Calvados. There was nothing to eat except for sandwiches and greasy quiche, and the rapid way my mind was turning over would keep me from getting drunk.

I shook my head. How had I managed to stand working with Chen for so long? If I could only nail him once and for all! I could almost feel Commander Youssef's hand on my shoulder and hear his words. 'Well done, Schwarzwald. I'm very grateful to you. What Wu might have done if you hadn't picked up his trail doesn't bear thinking of.'

Yes, and a lot of people at Central Office would be grateful. There was hardly one of our colleagues who Chen hadn't called a 'careerist', a 'creep', a 'corrupt arse-hole', 'enough to make you sick' or 'a heart amputee'. All of them favourite expressions of Chen – the man who knew how to have an argument! 'Heart amputee' in particular always surprised me. How could a man who obviously had no heart for anyone or anything at all (except perhaps for a night with a young woman all tarted up but on closer inspection perfectly ordinary, like the one on the park bench), how could a man like that think up such an insult? It was probably what they call projection.

'Excuse me, Monsieur, but I'm closing in a minute. If you'd like to pay, please.' The café owner put down a plastic plate with my bill on it.

'Of course.' I reached for my wallet. In the park opposite,

Chen was still on his knees in the flower bed, planting roses and talking to the woman. It was now ten-fifteen. Although I knew the Boulevard Richard Lenoir very well, and for a short stretch it even bordered my own area of operations, at this moment I couldn't think of a bar or brasserie likely to be open at this time of night near the Bastille end of the boulevard. I didn't fancy the prospect of having to lurk in the entrance of some building. In addition, I was feeling the effects of the Calvados, and my desire to unmask Chen as soon as possible was getting stronger all the time. That's the only way I can explain how I came to make such a stupid mistake.

'Tell me,' I said to the café owner in a deliberately casual voice and with a heavy German accent, as I put my money on the plate, 'is there another bar with a view of that lovely little park over there, a bar that would be open at this time of night? I'm a town planner, I come from Germany, we don't see parks like that much at home.'

The café owner, who had been wiping down the counter, stopped in mid-movement and looked at me, frowning. I remembered his unfriendly glance earlier, and even before he could reply I guessed what was coming, and froze. This café was much too close to Chez Max.

'Town planner,' said the man. 'Well, that's a good one!'

The expression on his face didn't tell me how he meant it, and I had no alternative but to smile gormlessly and hope my presentiment was wrong. My hopes were in vain.

'In that case,' he said, 'I needn't have spent a king's ransom on three tiny meatballs in piquant sauce at your place the other day. But my wife was dead set on going to

100

that smart German restaurant for once.'

I just went on smiling. Perhaps he'd think better of it. After all, I was his customer.

'So now the restaurateur who only recently shook my hand as I left comes into my own café, keeps watching our gardener and his girlfriend all the time, and tries to tell me he's a town planner from Germany. Talk about weird.'

'Listen ...'

But he wouldn't let me get a word in. 'Either this is something to do with Wu's girlfriend, even if you seem to me a little old for the part of jealous husband, or ...' He looked me up and down, my glasses with the lenses that were rather too thick, my unobtrusive clothes, my comfortable shoes, 'or you're a snoop. One of that lot.' He gestured in the direction of the Eiffel Tower.

Even though the Ashcroft Central Office was camouflaged as a scientific institute, and in part of the building several research labs did in fact work on ways to extract energy from the earth's core, most of the population of Paris knew or guessed who was really based there. Not that people talked about it. Certainly not to someone thought to be one of its employees. The café owner had definitely gone too far.

My expression froze. Without taking my eyes off the man, I took off my binocular-lensed glasses, placed them slowly in their case and put them away in my jacket pocket.

I let a couple more seconds pass before saying, in a menacingly quiet tone of voice, 'One of what lot?'

The café owner, who had held my eyes until now, looked away. He obviously realized what might be in store for him if I really was an Ashcroft man.

'And suppose I *was* "one of that lot", who do you

imagine *you* are? Maybe someone whose miserable little café can't be closed down double quick? Who can't have any tax dodges or infringements of the hygiene regulations proved against him? Who can simply break the social contract with impunity? Since when does anyone talk about the people over there,' I concluded, gesturing to the Eiffel Tower as he had done, 'as if they were the dregs of society?'

'I didn't mean it like …'

'Keep quiet.'

He bit his lip.

I was in full flow now. It wasn't only that this was a way for me to work off the pressure that had built up over the last few hours – above all, I had to put enough of the fear of God into the man to keep him from going straight to 'our gardener' and telling him about me. All I needed was for Chen to hear that the proprietor of Chez Max was probably an Ashcroft man and was after him.

'And what do you mean, "our gardener"? Do you pay his wages? No, the state pays them. The same state whose employees look after our security, though you describe them as snoops.'

'I only meant …'

'So why "our gardener"?'

Admittedly that wasn't just a peg to hang something on in order intimidate him. It annoyed me to find that it sounded as if in this sphere at least, Chen was an accepted or even popular member of society. I'd never heard anyone say of me 'our restaurateur' or 'our German'. (Or only one man, and he was the one I'd had jailed for a few cigarettes.)

'Well, because that's what he is,' said the café owner in an anxious but slightly surprised tone of voice. 'I mean, he's our gardener in this part of the city. He just belongs here. I've known him quite a while. He often has his coffee in here. A nice guy.'

A nice guy. It wasn't the first time I'd heard that Chen found it easy to make friends with ordinary people, after a fashion. Of course it was all just a trick. In reality, he probably thought the café owner a primitive proletarian. I'd have liked to tell him who that nice guy actually was: not just one of the 'snoops' he disliked, but a terrorist, a man who despised the human race if ever I saw one. But blowing a colleague's cover was punishable by a prison sentence of no less than two years. And Chen was still my colleague. I pulled myself together.

'A nice guy. If I were one of "that lot",' I said, pointing to the Eiffel Tower again, 'do you think I'd go spying on a nice guy?'

The café owner was visibly squirming with discomfort. 'Well, I'm sure you'd have your reasons. I mean, I hardly know Wu. But he's always friendly to me. However, I've heard here in the café how he can be rather nasty to other people.'

'Nasty in what way?'

'Well …' He looked at the floor. 'If he thinks they're talking twaddle. Repeating something parrot-fashion, truisms of some kind or what they read in the papers. If they talk big and act as if they know all sorts of stuff. For instance, once he lost his temper because someone said something – I can't remember what – was the truth. "The truth!" Wu snapped at him. "*A* truth or *your* truth, but not *the* truth – what a fool."'

That sounded much more like the Chen I knew.

'I guess,' said the café owner, glancing briefly at me, 'that could be one reason the state security services might be interested in him. Because he sometimes talks about political stuff.'

'Oh, does he?'

'Nothing actually forbidden, but now and then he brings up some very unusual subjects.'

'For instance?'

The café owner hesitated. He was nervously kneading his fingers. 'You won't close my café down, will you?'

I gave him a chilly smile. 'Who am I? How would I be in any position to do so? Forgotten already? I own the Chez Max. I'm a café proprietor like you. But of course, like any other citizen, I can go to the police if I notice anything wrong.'

He quickly glanced around: a reflex action. His café was as faded and grubby as many of its kind. And as in most of them, there were sure to be a few frozen dishes in the storeroom freezers which were past their eat-by date, or some mould in a fridge, if not even a crate of spirits with a forged brand name.

'Well?'

He kneaded his fingers again, staring straight ahead of him as if looking down a hole.

'… it's really only that he – well, normally nobody talks about the countries the other side of the Fence and life there. But Wu does. He doesn't give any opinion or suchlike, he just says certain things are fact.'

'The truth,' I derisively suggested.

'I don't know. I guess he just tries to see things the way they are. For instance, he once said – seeing we're talking about the truth – he said how that brown sugar there, you have it in your own restaurant to go with coffee too …'

He tried a conspiratorial smile. The attempt failed dismally.

'Well, anyway, that sugar, the kind everyone says is the best and healthiest, Wu once listed all the people it wouldn't be good for, he said it could sometimes be lethal.'

'Lethal sugar?' I laughed briefly. As I did so I looked across at the park. Chen had risen to his feet and was knocking the earth off his trousers.

'He said how in the sugarcane plantations or in the factories it must be, like, back-breaking work. And of course all the plants are sprayed, and the workers are always in contact with that poisonous stuff. And seems like they get very low pay, they live in huts without running water and all that – almost like slaves. Well, so then if their truth about brown sugar is different from ours, that makes sense.' The man looked up, saw my expressionless face, and hastily added, 'I mean, I don't have any idea myself, that's just what Wu said. And I'm not really interested. I'm only telling you so you'll know the way he sometimes talks.'

There was no end to Chen's surprises. Here he was, publicly engaging in agitation and discussion of the Second World! Had he no scruples at all? No conscience? No sense of common decency? Because of course the sugarcane story was sheer propaganda, a fairy tale. And because Chen couldn't know the first thing about working conditions on the Caribbean islands. And the reason for that was that no one knew anything about them, for the islands had been a quarantined area ever since repeated epidemics of Bodo disease had broken out there, killing thousands. I myself had heard about it only because I knew someone who worked in the Health Ministry. The Bodo virus, for which no treatment had yet been found, attacked the gastro-intestinal tract and led to over eighty per cent of victims literally puking themselves to death within a few weeks. The only certain thing was that the sugar itself didn't carry the virus, and our supplies were thus secure for now. All the same, the state laboratories were working flat out in their search for a vaccine, while the local authorities were doing all they could, as my acquaintance put it, to protect and care for the native population. Special clothing and face masks were being distributed, water pipes were being laid even in the most remote villages, and centres known as Welcome Camps had been set up, where the last weeks of the lives of the infected were made as tolerable as possible with films, concerts and computer games.

Lethal sugar – if the subject hadn't been so serious, I'd have laughed out loud.

I looked out of the window again. Chen had put his spade and bucket in a wheelbarrow and, with the woman, was turning to go.

I turned to the bar counter and looked hard into the café owner's eyes.

'I have to leave now. You'll forget our little talk, is that clear?'

'Of course.'

'Because if I ever hear that you've been saying anything about this to anyone at all, or that you ever expressed a certain suspicion in connection with me, then …' and here I leaned towards the window and read the name of the café in lights on the neon sign above the door '… then it'll be curtains for La Palombe. And I get to hear a lot.'

'I should think you do,' said the café owner, with awe in his voice.

'Thinking is exactly what we don't want you doing. You're not to think anything about me, you're to forget me.' I picked up the glass sugar-caster from the bar. 'And to make sure you understand that …' I swung my arm back and threw the sugar-caster into the array of spirits lined up in front of a mirror on the wall. Bottles and bits of broken mirror-glass crashed to the floor, as the café owner jumped out of the way in alarm. 'Understand? That was your shelf of spirits, and your life is just as fragile.'

Then I turned and hurried out of the café. Outside, I saw Chen pushing the wheelbarrow ahead of him, walking slowly down the boulevard with the woman towards the Bastille. He had his tool-shed somewhere there.

I followed them under cover of the trees and shrubs. As I passed the flowerbed that Chen had been planting, I stopped and looked at the result of his labours, feeling oddly moved. The red roses were planted in the shape of a heart, and the name 'Natalia' was written in the middle of it in daisies.

Twenty minutes later I was hiding behind an advertising billboard near Père Lachaise, watching Chen on the other side of the road giving an order in a Vietnamese restaurant with a takeaway service. The woman – Natalia, I assumed – was standing close to him, nodding to everything he showed her on the menu.

As they waited for the food to arrive Natalia moved away from him, went to the door of the restaurant, stepped out into the street and glanced around. She was probably looking for a wine merchant. Perhaps she didn't fancy cheap Asian beer.

I quickly felt in my pockets for the contact lenses with the built-in camera. But I must have left them at Chez

Max, and all I had on me that I could use to take her picture was the sexomat shooter. I felt a little uncomfortable about that, but I knew it was for purely professional reasons, after all.

Keeping it under my jacket, I set the shooter to a distance of fifteen to twenty metres away, held it at half-height beside the billboard, got Natalia in the viewfinder, and pressed the Shoot button. I filmed her as she clattered a little way down the street on her high heels, looked down the next side street, turned and went back to the restaurant.

I automatically glanced at the time and movement gauge. Natalia had been in the picture for over a minute, and the sexomat would be able to reproduce seventy-three per cent of her possible movements. But of course that didn't interest me. I only needed her face. I was going to feed it into the Ashcroft computer and find out if she had ever come to our attention for forbidden political activities or showing sympathy with terrorist groups.

A little later the two of them left the restaurant with a bag full of food containers, and went hand in hand towards Chen's apartment. Chen was still wearing his work clothes, and Natalia's high heels made her a little taller than he was. An odd couple. Beauty and the Beast. Not that Natalia, so far as I could conclude from my observations, was my type – I preferred self-assured women, women of character who ordered their own food and didn't lie down, so to speak, in front of a man's bedroom door in their clickety-clack heels and clothes saying *ooh, here I am, eat me all up!* All the same, there was no denying that objectively speaking Natalia was attractive, in the same way as, objectively speaking, Chen was a little slitty-eyes wearing trousers caked with mud. Extraordinary.

Outside Chen's apartment building, there was a front garden with a gravel path leading through it. As the two of them went towards the door, I was standing about twenty metres away behind a refuse separator. Chen suddenly bent down, picked up a handful of gravel, turned towards the street and threw it my way. I ducked, the gravel hit the refuse separator and the parked bicycles. Natalia laughed.

What was that stupid stuff for? To impress her? But Chen was too old for such things. Or had Natalia perhaps said, 'This is a really posh pad you live in!' That would have matched her garish get-up. On seeing something really tasteful and stylish – and you couldn't describe the nine-teenth-century architecture of the building where Chen lived as anything else – the common suburban princess, hairdresser or tanning salon hostess by trade with dreams of a career as a film star and her own home could resort only to a silly adolescent pose and call it a 'posh pad' on account of her lack of education and culture. And Chen, his brain totally flooded by testosterone, would cheerfully go along with her and say something like, 'Yes, how about we wake up the stuffed shirts who live here?' Whereupon Natalia would go into fits of laughter and say, 'Man, are you ever crazy!'

What an undignified exchange!

When I leaned forward again, the two of them had disappeared. Soon after that the light went on in Chen's apartment. I saw him appear at the window two or three times, and once I had a feeling that he was looking straight at me. I ducked back behind the refuse separator. Then he drew the curtains, and the light inside changed as if they'd lit some candles.

I watched the shadows moving back and forth behind the curtains for a while, until they too disappeared, and an odd feeling overcame me: incredulity at first, then an increasingly empty sense of depression.

So that was it for today. No haul of 'diamonds', no sighting of Chen meeting any suspiciously Middle Eastern characters, and no busy preparations to move the illegals.

Instead I suddenly saw myself, lurking alone and rather pointlessly behind a refuse separator, my shoes in a foaming puddle, the smell of the bio-refuse bin in my nostrils. And up there Chen was having a good time.

I stepped out of the puddle and wiped my shoes on a strip of grass. But of course his conduct was an almost perfect imitation of Björn Hallsund: ice-cold, brazen, ignorant. He acted in the firm belief that all the rest of the human race were fools. How else could he simply go to bed with a girlfriend on an evening like this? Suppose the TFSP had finally had enough of it, picked up the illegals and subjected them to high-urgency interrogation? Within half an hour they'd have a description of the Iranians' Chinese contact man. Blowing yourself sky-high was one thing, quick and presumably painless, standing up to a high-pressure interrogation was something else.

But his very ignorance, I felt sure, would finally be Chen's downfall. I just had to hope the TFSP people wouldn't snap this titbit up from under my nose.

On the way home I stopped at Le Canard and bought myself an artichoke sandwich with a thick slice of *foie gras* and truffles. *A festival for the taste buds*, as the ad for the famous bistro put it. I felt I'd earned it.

Chapter 5

Next morning I was standing in the interior courtyard of Chez Max with Alexi, one of my waiters, a young man in his early twenties, examining the ivy growing up the walls and now reaching the roof, where it was beginning to raise and shift some tiles.

I had a hangover. It had taken me a long time to calm down last night, and once home I'd drunk two bottles of Franconian wine before I was finally able to get to sleep. All the same, I had woken at seven in the morning even without an alarm. After a quick breakfast I'd called Alexi, got him out of bed, and asked him to come in early to get the courtyard in order. Of course it could have been put off until next day or next week, but I had to stay at Chez Max until we began serving lunch, and I was too nervous just to sit around or to concentrate on paperwork and the accounts. I could hardly wait to carry on shadowing Chen, and until then I thought it would be a good idea to occupy my mind with something practical like the ivy.

'Boss, why is our fish soup called Soup Günter? There was a customer asked me that again yesterday.'

'It's the first name of a German winner of the Nobel Prize for Literature. The recipe was his.'

'When did he live, then?'

'Beginning of the century.'

The ivy had to go. The problem was that over the years the stems, some of them by now up to twenty centimetres thick, had practically grown into the natural stone walls and merged with them. We weren't getting anywhere with the saw we'd borrowed from a neighbour.

'For literature?' said Alexi, yawning. His hair was still untidy from his night's sleep. 'Kind of a shame he's only remembered for a soup recipe, then.'

'He isn't.'

Alexi thought about it. He was a nice lad, but not all that bright.

'Someone was asking about it, though,' he finally said.

'We need an axe.'

'Yup.'

'Right. You go round to the garden centre and buy one.'

'Maybe we could borrow one from next door.'

'Kindly just go and buy one!'

Alexi gave me a funny look. I didn't know myself exactly why I wanted an axe of our own, but I did. Surely Chez Max could afford its own axe!

'Go on, get moving.'

'Okay, boss.'

When Alexi had left I went into the restaurant and made myself a double espresso behind the bar. As I did, I was thinking of the surprised look on Alexi's face when I insisted on buying the axe. Had I sounded impatient, even angry? I mean, was wanting to buy an axe anything out of the ordinary?

It was probably just the typical Ashcroft reflex, which was to regard any action as suspicious if there was no obvious reason for it – but I suddenly thought I ought to come up with a more plausible explanation than simply saying that Chez Max could afford its own axe.

And it didn't take me long to think of one either: I

certainly didn't want to start any rumours that we had to scrimp and save over even the smallest purchases. Of course, this was rubbish. On the other hand, our takings at Chez Max had been steadily dropping for over a year now, and my waking nightmare from the evening before was still weighing on my mind.

When I'd come home from shadowing Chen, and after I had indulged myself for a while, over that Franconian wine, imagining how different, how easy life without Chen would be, the balance of the whole thing had suddenly shifted. All at once I was thinking about sharing duties in Quadrate 3 of the eleventh arrondissement with a new partner, one who couldn't be expected to achieve such a high quota as Chen's or anywhere near it. And that could mean I'd be on the way out myself. Because in the eyes of our colleagues and superiors I was, without a doubt, the quiet force at Chen's side who always represented the voice of reason, thus making his success possible in the first place. Of course, for a while I could live on my reputation as the man who unmasked Super-Chen, but how long would that last? Within a few months Commander Youssef was bound to remember our successful operations of the past. And at some point he might say, 'I'm sorry, Schwarzwald, but it looks as if you're not much good to us without Chen. Why don't you think of taking early retirement?' Which would mean closing down Chez Max, because without my Ashcroft subsidy for setting up and maintaining a convincing long-term façade, I couldn't keep the restaurant with its twelve permanent employees going.

And that nightmare hadn't surfaced in my mind out of nowhere, either. A few weeks ago Youssef had summoned me to his office.

'Listen, Schwarzwald,' he had said, coming straight to the point, 'considering that Wu is your partner, your own operational success rate may never look particularly good, but I think you're letting things slide a bit at the moment.'

It was like a slap in the face. Youssef didn't have the reputation of being especially picky, nor was he considered a really tough guy. Far from it: he generally let things take their course, left us to do our work in whatever way we thought right, and intervened only when he feared that the conduct of an individual might damage the department's good name. Most people saw him as being in full command. Myself, I was more inclined to share the opinion of Chen, who had once said, 'Youssef has a seaside villa in Perpignan, a pretty wife, and two more years to go until retirement. So he's not going to let any kind of shit upset him.'

'I'm sorry, Commander, but over these last few weeks I've had ...'

'Don't give me reasons, please,' he interrupted me. 'In the last month alone, inhabitants of your area have murdered one man, raped two women, and raided two business premises – and you didn't give me so much as a word of warning about the perpetrators of any of those crimes.'

'But it's been proved that the murder was committed in a moment of strong emotion, and the rapist was only fifteen.'

'I said no reasons please. And what do you mean, he was only fifteen?'

'Well, he was still a child. You can say it's wrong of me, but when it comes to children I'm still convinced of the fundamental goodness of humanity.'

'Are you, indeed? How nice. And what do you think

those two women would say about it? Furthermore, your "child" was getting on for six foot tall, and only two months earlier he'd been caught giving a false age while trying to buy a sexomat. If you don't think that's enough to arouse suspicion ...'

A little later I had stepped out of Youssef's office, feeling dazed, and stopped at a bar on my way home. And my success rates hadn't improved since then either.

I stirred sugar into my espresso and thought: well, let's hope all that's about to change over the next few days.

At any rate, considering my smouldering existential fears of the last few months, it seemed to me only sensible to rule out any possibility that our neighbour might go around saying we were always borrowing tools from him, just as if we were penniless students or sub-tenants.

The axe had a handle about fifty centimetres long, and its blade was sharp as a knife.

'Go carefully,' I told Alexi as he started hacking at the ivy stems. 'And then dig out as much of the roots as you can.'

Alexi let the axe drop and looked up at the walls of our inner courtyard. 'I kind of feel there ought to be something growing here, all the same. I think the walls will look very bare without that ivy.'

I nodded. 'Yes, I was thinking of Virginia creeper or wisteria instead. And perhaps a few climbing roses.'

'Oh, sure,' he said. 'And we could plant olive or lemon trees in the corners. It never gets too cold for them here in the courtyard. Or little bay trees, bay always smells nice and it keeps its leaves in winter. If you like – well, a friend of mine is a gardener, I could ask him some time.'

'Thanks, Alexi, but …' I hesitated. A totally absurd idea had just occurred to me. Or maybe it wasn't so absurd after all? When I came to think of it – why not at least take advantage of knowing Chen for once? Yes, it was a little macabre just before I was going to expose him, but did the two really have anything to do with each other? Chen was still a gardener, a good one too, and he could hardly refuse to design me a planting plan for the court-yard. I almost grinned gleefully: so at the very end of our partnership we'd for once be working almost as a team for an afternoon. Not that I seriously imagined it, let alone wanted it, but perhaps it wouldn't have been entirely unthinkable if Chen hadn't said, on our first meeting four years ago, 'Oh, and all that teamwork guff, it doesn't work with me.'

'Teamwork guff?'

'You know what I mean: shadowing suspects together, hanging around in some café waiting for something, putting on a big double act in front of the suspects – I'd really rather have as little as possible to do with your area.'

'Okay.'

To Alexi, I said, 'As it happens I know a gardener myself. An old acquaintance of mine. He'll do it for free.'

'Oh, that's all right, then.'

Once again he looked as if there was something unusual about my behaviour. This time I couldn't help myself. 'What are you looking at me like that for?'

He started slightly. 'Oh, no reason.'

'Come on, tell me.'

'It's just that … you seem so absent-minded today. But I guess you're just over-tired. All that business can't have been easy for you.'

'All what business?'

'Well, I mean your friend being arrested and all. The painter. It must have come as quite a shock. And him going behind your back too. I've heard he kind of ran his sales from the restaurant. It's not fair to go dragging your friends into a thing like that.'

I couldn't think what to say in reply.

'Anyway, I'd have thought he could just as well have done his drug dealing in one of the cafés down on the boulevard, instead of giving your restaurant a bad name.'

'What do you mean, a bad name?'

'Well, people talk, of course. And there's a whole lot of artists and suchlike come here – but if you mention Chez Max these days, everyone comes out with stories about wild parties and sniffing coke.'

'Really?' I asked in surprise.

Alexi leaned forward, lowering his voice, and said, 'So that's why I'm pretty sure that one of that lot over there …' and he pointed in the direction of the Eiffel Tower, '… comes in here to eat quite often.'

'Hm. Yes, I see.' I nodded. 'Well, no need for us to worry about that. After all, we don't have wild parties here, or coke-sniffing either.'

'Be careful, boss. If they want to catch someone at it, they'll find something. For instance, your friend,' he was almost whispering now, 'I've heard from other people that all he really did was smoke a cigarette now and then.'

'Oh, come on, Alexi,' I snapped. 'First you tell me how unfair it was of Leon to peddle his drugs in my restaurant, now you suddenly say he only smoked occasional cigarettes.'

'I don't know which is right, boss. I'm only saying, mind your back. It would be too bad if anything happened to Chez Max.'

Too bad! I repeated that in my head.

'Thanks, Alexi. But now would you get to work on that ivy? I'd like to see the first wall cleared by the time we start serving lunch.'

I made myself another espresso in the restaurant, and after I'd made sure that Alexi couldn't see me I added a shot of Calvados.

So Leon's arrest was a subject of conversation around here. Of course that wasn't so surprising, particularly not after the attention the TEF had attracted. Once this Chen business was over, I'd find out who was responsible for that. Probably some young rookie who liked to talk big – 'Hey, let's try out our super new jalopy!'

I tipped the espresso and Calvados down my throat. I felt a pang every time I thought of Leon. What terrible timing! If only I'd found out about Chen's links with terrorism a week earlier, I'd never have grassed on Leon. What did catching one little potential drug dealer mean compared to unmasking Chen? And I certainly wouldn't have been the first Ashcroft agent to stop a friend doing something stupid with a few quiet words of warning.

Well, there was no way I could change things now. But that made it all the more important to catch Chen. Obviously that wasn't a logical train of thought, really just more of a feeling that nabbing Chen was, in a way, a kind of apology for turning Leon in. Or at least Leon's arrest could be seen in a wider, more important context than just an unsuccessful artist looking for a way out of his financial difficulties, and an unsuccessful Ashcroft agent needing to up his success rate. Maybe Leon's arrest, leaving me under great emotional and mental pressure, was what I needed to help me see through Chen?

I looked at the glass door to the courtyard, and when I heard Alexi hacking away I poured myself another Calvados.

Or was there something else at work inside me, something quite different? A strange, unjust, unfathomable secret feeling that I didn't want to know about? A feeling that scared even me? So much so that I didn't dare to think it out clearly?

I emptied the cup of Calvados in a single draught.

If so, then my feeling was unjust! Couldn't that happen to anyone? Wasn't I a human being? Wasn't I allowed to have feelings? And were feelings always just? What's more, whether or not I had such a feeling, it didn't alter anything for anyone. It was simply there, inside me. And there inside me it said: Chen must pay for Leon's arrest! Or in other words: if Leon was in jail, and it was my doing, I couldn't let a man like Chen run around free!

I stopped my thoughts short, then suddenly smiled with relief, and next moment I shook my head. Tormenting myself like this! Over nothing but an understandable if childish wish to make up for something done wrong by doing something right.

What a little bleeding heart I was! Chen would have laughed himself silly at me – and then gone back to strapping explosives to suicide bombers.

Soon afterwards the butcher delivered fresh black pudding and liver sausage. A little later Ravelli the head chef and Maurice the kitchen assistant arrived. I discussed the lunch menu with Ravelli – a dozen raw mussels as a starter, then the two kinds of sausage served with sauerkraut and new potatoes, a lavender cream for dessert – and

I invented an appointment which was going to keep me away from the restaurant all afternoon and probably all evening too.

'On the trail, boss?' asked Ravelli, grinning. 'The fox hunting chickens again?'

'Hmhm,' I said, putting on my knowing smile that said a gentleman kisses but never tells. And I left the kitchen.

Sometimes I wondered whether my staff laughed at me behind my back. But I couldn't really imagine it. They were all nice lads, and they were well off working for me. And who'd risk getting on the wrong side of his boss for the sake of a joke? They probably really did think I was a bit of a playboy, and to be honest I liked the idea of that a lot better than if they'd shown that they were concerned about my private life, or even pitied me.

By now there was a large heap of hacked-off ivy in the middle of the courtyard, and Alexi had almost cleared two of the four walls.

'It was worth buying that axe,' I called from the doorway.

Alexi turned, wiped the sweat from his forehead, and said appreciatively, 'That's one hell of a tool! You could split a cow with it!'

Split a cow? What on earth made him think of that?

'Well, mind you don't hurt yourself. And when you're through, leave the axe …' I thought for a moment. 'You'd better leave it over there behind the barbecue. Not that anyone's going to find it and do something silly with it.'

'What kind of something silly, boss?'

'Well …' The questions that lad asked! 'Well, you said yourself you could split a cow with it. Suppose a customer's had too much to drink – anyway, I don't want the axe simply lying around, understand?'

'Sure, boss. I'll leave it behind the barbecue.'

I cast a brief glance around the dining room. The kitchen assistant had laid the tables now, everything was as it should be, and I wished Ravelli and the boy good luck for lunchtime.

When I had gone out into the stairwell through the back door, I stood still for a moment, breathing deeply. This was it. Everything inside me said that I was going to bring Chen down today.

Chapter 6

My apartment was right above Chez Max. I'd negotiated the whole set-up over fifteen years ago when the Ashcroft recruiting officers approached me. After countless spells as a waiter, snack-bar manager and chef, I wanted my own restaurant, plus an apartment, and I already knew the very place for it. How often I'd sat under the plane trees in the quiet park on the Rue du Général Guilhem during my free time, looking up at the well-maintained, attractively decorated old building, thinking: what a wonderful place for an elegant restaurant, slightly out of the way, and how good it would be to live right above it. Max Schwarzwald's own little kingdom.

I signed on for life with the Ashcroft agency, and two weeks later renovation work began on the rooms of the former laundry on the ground floor.

Now, as I closed the door of the apartment behind me, I thought briefly of the feelings that had buoyed me up back then. My professional dream was well on the way to fulfilment. I had a first-class apartment in an excellent part of town, and I was doing society a valuable service. All of a sudden I wasn't just a successful man, I was a good man too. The Ashcroft agency had given higher meaning to my life. I wasn't just chasing around after money, success and sex any more like everyone else, I was one of those who put their best efforts into providing peace and security for mankind.

Of course that feeling faded over the years, everyday life caught up with me, new worries came along – that's the way it goes. But at this moment I suddenly felt something of the old idealism and euphoria of my first weeks again. I could hardly wait to put myself to the service of society once more. At the same time, I wasn't kidding myself: in this case the interests of society coincided directly with my own. But wasn't it always like that for an Ashcroft agent? Wasn't my own good a part of the general good, and vice versa? Wasn't a good man on a mission always on a mission for everyone else too?

I hung my jacket on the coat-stand and set to work.

I packed a toolbox with various bugging devices, a movement detector, a Set Day & Night mini-camera, a jemmy and KO gas. Then I put on a blue overall, big boots and an orange cap, the sort worn by electricity workers. A disguise I'd never used before.

After that I went over to my office. The sexomat shooter was still lying on the desk. The sight of it, and remembering that last night I really had used it only to check up on Natalia's identity, nothing more, filled me with pride for a moment.

The check hadn't come up with much: Natalia was single, worked in publicity for a sportswear business, lived in a three-room apartment in the eighth arrondissement. I found no crimes or suspicions of potential crime in her Ashcroft file. She had never been in conflict with the law, and the only connection she had with the other side of the Fence was the family of an uncle three times removed living somewhere in Mongolia. Very likely she knew nothing at all about him. Apart from that, she was good at her job, played tennis in her leisure time, liked to go dancing in the evenings, had a cat, and usually spent her holidays by the Black Sea. Her family came from Odessa.

I don't know why, but somewhere at the back of my head I'd been expecting something more exciting from Chen.

I picked up the shooter, went into the living-room and put it away with the suit and the other sexomat accessories in the hiding-place behind the sofa. Then I sat down at the desk and called the number of the Ashcroft Localization Office. Asking for someone to be located for the second time within twenty-four hours was rather tricky, but I had no other option. Anyway, if Chen's phone hadn't been working yesterday, why wouldn't it simply be broken?

'Ashcroft Localization Office, my name is Rosental,' said a chirpy young female voice, like the evening before – maybe, I thought, I ought to pay the Localization Office a visit in person some time. 'May I have your voice identification, please?'

I said, 'Liberté, égalité, sécurité'.

A few seconds passed. 'Monsieur Schwarzwald, good morning, how may I help you?'

'Good morning. I'm looking for my partner Chen Wu, eleventh arrondissement.'

'Would you give your reasons, please?'

'I called you yesterday evening – this is still about a group of illegals in a building in our area of operations. The problem is, Wu's telephone is out of order. He was going to get it repaired this morning but ... well, you know how it goes. Anyway, something has just occurred in connection with those illegals, and I need to speak to him as a matter of urgency.'

'I must inform you that your reasons are being recorded for the files.'

'Of course.'

Another few seconds passed. 'Oh, Monsieur Schwarz-wald ...'

'Yes?'

'We don't need any reasons. I've just seen that your partner took a look at his localization records this morning, and gave us permission to tell you his where-abouts at any time.'

'But what ...?'

'Well, I suppose that's because he's having his phone checked, just like you thought. However, I must ask both of you not to use our office for making contact except in really urgent cases. Why don't you simply borrow a phone from somewhere?'

'Because I ... well, sure ... please tell me where Wu is at this moment. It really is a matter of ...'

I was finding it hard to speak clearly. My gums suddenly felt as if they were made of an egg-box.

'Very well, Monsieur Schwarzwald, but do please think of getting a substitute telephone. We are really not respon-sible for your present situation. Well ... do you have a pen there?'

'Tell me the address, please.'

She told me the address, establishing the precise point where Chen now was with reference to a north-south system and metrical data, and added, 'Oh, and I almost forgot. He's on the first floor.'

She didn't need to tell me so.

At that very moment a voice behind me said, 'Here I am, you arsehole.'

For several seconds I felt as if everything was going black before my eyes, and then somehow I managed to press the key to end the connection and put my phone down on the desk. Then I slowly turned in my chair. Chen was leaning in the doorway, hands casually dug into his trouser pockets, smiling that innocently friendly Chen smile of his, the one that he generally used to underline particularly exquisite flights of bad language.

'Oh,' I said, and tried to get some saliva into my dry mouth. 'I was just ... well, what a coincidence. But what are you doing here? And how did you get in?'

'Through the door.'

'I ... ah ... er ...'

'We learn that kind of thing in our job, right? Or most of us do,' said Chen, with a slightly friendlier smile. 'Although there are some who'd rather lurk behind dustbins down at street level and hope for something to happen.'

'Behind dustbins ...' I was trying to sound amused.

'Exactly,' he said, pausing and looking at me curiously. I was experiencing some difficulty in breathing.

Then, as if he were honestly interested in the answer, he added, 'What did you think when I threw those pebbles at you? Nothing at all? Sometimes people do go throwing stones around the place? Or maybe: oh Lord, there goes Chen fucking about again?'

'I ... I really don't know what ...'

'My girlfriend thought there was some pervert following us. But I'd already seen my good friend Max passing us in such a brilliantly inconspicuous way in the park. Did you learn that at some Ashcroft training course? Look away from the subject you're shadowing as if you were suddenly struck with paralysis? And then go and sit in a brightly lit café and try to stare the subject down?'

He looked at me expectantly. 'Well, what *were* you thinking about?'

'Please, Chen …' All at once I felt so weak that I would have liked just to close my eyes and go limp. 'Honestly I can explain it …'

'Go on, then.'

'Well, for a start …' I looked at the floor. I had to pull myself together, I had to concentrate, think … My God, this was all going wrong!

'I wasn't shadowing you – at least, not hoping to catch you out at something, I simply …. Well, I wanted to be sure you weren't going to do anything stupid …'

'Fancy that!'

I nodded, without looking up from the floor. 'You have no idea … I mean …'

And suddenly, as if under all that pressure a curtain had been drawn aside or a door had swung open, I saw the way out. Or rather, I saw how things were. Or how they could have been. Because how could he have guessed that I'd known the truth about him since yesterday, that the Hallsund story had put me on his trail? Outwardly, everything was just fine. I hadn't said a word to give myself away. I just had to keep calm and find my way out of this fix.

Raising my head, I said in a reasonably firm voice, 'The TFSP got in touch with me directly after our conversation yesterday. It turned out that they were shadowing the illegals mainly because of you, kind of on behalf of Self-Protection. Self-Protection wants to know about some kind of offence that can be pinned on you, so they'll have leverage against you.'

'Oh yes? What kind of offence?'

'Well … they don't seem to know precisely what themselves. But I think they suspect you of letting illegals go now and then. Or maybe even of something more serious.'

'Something more serious?'

'Well, perhaps of hiding the Iranians yourself. I mean ...' I paused for a moment, and felt that I was getting myself better under control all the time. 'Remember, what you say about the state of the world is known in-house, and of course Self-Protection know about it too. That's why they want something that they can hold against you. To make sure you keep quiet in future. For instance, when you said in the canteen the other day that the TFSP posted firing squads by the Fence – that upset certain people quite a lot.'

Chen shrugged his shoulders. As he did so, I registered the fact that his smile had disappeared. He was even looking thoughtful. For the first time since he'd turned up I felt my tension relax a little, and simultaneously I had to work hard to hide the hatred rising in me. This must be something like the way the Border officials had felt about Hallsund when, in spite of knowing that he was fooling them and in spite of the names he called them, they had no option but to keep a civil tongue in their heads and crawl to him.

'At least it's not too far-fetched to suppose, in that connection, that you sometimes follow up your words with deeds.'

'Hmhm. Why did you call the Localization Office?'

'Well, I thought if they were after you, they'd probably be bugging your phone.' I had been expecting that question, and secretly I felt a little triumphant. 'Really, Chen, you must believe me. Yesterday evening I just wanted to make sure there was nothing in the TFSP's suspicions. And of course there wasn't. I saw you walking home with your girlfriend. If you were really involved with hiding the illegals, then ...' I let the sentence trail off, unfinished.

'You mean I'd have chased off in panic to do something?'

'Well ... after you'd heard about the surveillance from me, that would have been the obvious reaction.'

Chen frowned, then pushed himself away from the doorframe and began slowly walking up and down the room. As he did so he looked around attentively, noticing what was on my desk, looking at the shelves, reading the titles of books and the labelling of files, leafing through papers, even bending down to look in the bottom compartments of the shelving unit.

I made an effort to appear mildly annoyed by this invasion of my private space. But I was thinking: he doesn't know what to do next! He's just putting on an investigator's usual show. That's the only thing he can think of now.

Finally he stopped in the middle of the room, hands back in his trouser pockets – although the pose didn't look so casual now, it was more as if he didn't know what to do with his hands – turned to me and said, 'There's something wrong there.'

I looked attentive and injected sympathy into my voice. 'But Chen – please don't worry. It must have occurred to you that you're a thorn in Self-Protection's side. Well?' I leaned towards him. 'We'll get this sorted out between us. After all, I'm the best witness that there's no substance in such suspicions. On the contrary: you did the one right and proper thing – just as we'd expect from Super-Chen. You kept watch on the illegals in their hideout so that you could find the people-smugglers who got them in – full

stop. And even if you *had* intended to let the illegals go …
well, it's an open secret that you sometimes turn a blind
eye to those who can be regarded as social misfits rather
than criminals. And let me tell you something: above all,
there's your high reputation at the Ashcroft agency.
Imagine if you were only Chen the criminal-catching
machine! No, you still have a heart in spite of all your
success, that's what people admire in you – and if I may
say so, it's what I in particular admire in you.'

I heaved a small sigh and looked at him with deep
emotion, as if I hoped with all my heart that I had lifted a
little of the burden of anxiety from his shoulders.

Chen was looking disgusted, but I was used to that.
Then he took one hand out of his trouser pocket and
rubbed his eyes. When he took the hand away his expression was weary and somehow clouded.

'There's something wrong there,' he repeated. 'And
please stop spewing all that garbage. You're only putting a
strain on your imagination, and when you don't have
much of some commodity you want to use it sparingly.
Anyway, I don't believe a word of what you said. You were
following me yesterday, you were going to follow me
again today, and I assume you thought you could turn the
refugees into a rope to hang me with. I mean, you're well
known for what I might call the hole-and-corner manner
of your Ashcroft operations: friends, neighbours, your
Ashcroft partner – it's a wonder you haven't grassed on
any of your own staff yet. I'm sure one of them snaffles a
rump steak from time to time.'

He was still looking wearily at me, and perhaps it was
that expression in his eyes, but anyway, I wasn't afraid of
him any more. And at bottom what he said was only the
abuse I was accustomed to hearing from Chen. If he'd

really guessed what I knew about him, his approach would have been different. After all, everyone at Ashcroft knew he didn't shrink from physical violence in an argument. He'd twice set about colleagues, and the only thing that saved him had been witnesses saying those colleagues had been indulging in racist language. For what that was worth. Just think of all the comparisons with Hitler and the Gestapo that I'd had to put up with from him over the years …

And who was he to say I had no imagination? Chen's assessments were usually not entirely random, but in this case … well, if he'd had the faintest idea how much imagination I could summon up! Imagination had led me to the truth about him!

No doubt about it: Chen was down and out for the count. Which didn't necessarily mean he might not get up again quickly. I never knew with Chen. He might think of some way to corner me any moment. I had to get him out of my apartment.

In the same emotional tone as before, I said, 'I'm really sorry you think of me like that. I think we ought to have a serious talk about our partnership as soon as possible. We can't go on like this. However,' I said, looking at my watch, 'I have to get down to the restaurant for when we start serving lunch.' And although I hadn't thought of it before – it seemed obvious, or so I thought, that I ought to offer him some inducement to leave – I suggested, 'Why don't you come back here after three or thereabouts? I'll bring us up something nice to eat, and we'll try to settle all our misunderstandings at our leisure, how about that?' I smiled and raised my hands, shrugging, an ironically powerless gesture. 'I mean, we're still working partners, aren't we?'

I didn't often manage to take Chen by surprise, but I'd obviously done it this time. He was staring at me incredulously.

'And by the way,' I went on blithely, ' I was going to ask you to take a look at our inner courtyard some time anyway. We want to put some attractive climbing plants in, and I thought that as a gardener you might be able to help us. I know my request may come as a bit of a surprise just now, but …'

I was smiling again. Not a shred of malice in my head, a clear conscience, anxious to preserve harmony – good old simple-minded Max. I thought I could read Chen's thoughts in his face.

After a brief pause, he said, 'I hope you know what you're doing.'

'I know I'd like to get everything straightened out between us again.'

He shook his head. 'You're planning something, my dear Max. I've been in the business long enough to sense that. I really meant to go to Youssef now and tell him that my partner is spying on me. But don't worry, there's time enough for that, after all.' He cast me a fierce, challenging glance. 'First of all, I'd like to know if you're really dangerous. That would be something new – good old Max!'

'Dangerous …' What an absurd suspicion. And from Chen of all people! It was no effort for me to stare at him as if he were talking utter nonsense.

'Yes, well.' Chen dismissed it. 'See you later then, if you like. But think hard about what you're going to say to me about yesterday evening. I've never turned in a colleague yet, and to be honest I'd hate to do it, even with you. However, I have to know the truth. And you can leave out

all that nonsense about wanting to make sure I was innocent.'

He turned to the corridor and went a few steps before
turning round once more. 'Oh, and by the way, it *is* far-
fetched to say I follow up my words with deeds. I'm much
too comfortably off for that, probably too cowardly too.
But I'm not blind or stupid, I'm not entirely cynical
either. Above all, however, I'm an Ashcroft man. And if I
do now and then let a social misfit go, as you put it, that
doesn't mean I'd give any potential criminal a chance.' He
nodded to me. 'Don't forget that.'

I listened to him walking away, opening the door of the
apartment and closing it behind him. His footsteps echoed
on the stairs. For a while I waited in anxious expectation
of hearing those footsteps turn back again. At last I sank
back in my chair, exhausted, and stretched my legs.

Above all, however, I'm an Ashcroft man... what a joke!
The best evidence that he was *not* an Ashcroft man, but
was hiding something, lay in that very sentence. Since
when did Chen feel he had to explain himself to me? *I'm
much too comfortably off for that, probably too cowardly too.*
Chen as a law-abiding little cog in the wheel, nothing
more than a 'good cop' letting petty criminals off ... had
he forgotten that I'd heard him every week for years
emptying buckets full of hatred and criticism over our
world? And now, all of a sudden: *That doesn't mean I'd give
a potential criminal a chance.* Oh no? Even if I was by some
chance doing him an injustice with my Hallsund
comparison and he truly had no connection with any
suicide bombers – what, might I ask, was he but a potential terrorist himself, with his corrosive, coarse talk? He'd
be the perfect example of someone who so far had lacked
only the right opportunity.

But of course he *hadn't* lacked it. For one thing was certain: Chen would never have set things up to get into my apartment just to demand an explanation of why I'd been shadowing him. A man with a clear conscience wasn't bothered by a thing like that. And if he *was* bothered, why hadn't he gone straight to Youssef? That's what I'd have done in his place. And no doubt he hated me as much as I hated him. That meant he couldn't go to Youssef, and what he said just now had been an empty threat. Could I go to Youssef myself?

Not yet, I thought as I rose and went into the kitchen to pour myself a cognac. But maybe this evening. I'd simply tell Chen to his face, over our late lunch, what I thought, and I'd have a recorder running, and then we'd see! This time it was up to me to catch him on the hop. Today was by no means over yet.

I drained the glass, went into my bedroom and changed the coverall and boots for a pale brown suit and beige suede shoes. I planted a bug on myself in the tool room.

When I appeared in Chez Max a moment later, Ravelli greeted me with, 'Hi, boss! Has the pretty chicken flown the coop?'

'She's still preening her feathers, Ravelli. Set two good servings of that sausage and sauerkraut aside, would you?'

Just before two I saw the last customers off. Half an hour later the dining-room was cleared and swept, and the dishes were in the dishwasher.

I was sitting at a table near the glazed door that led to the courtyard, drinking a glass of white wine and wondering how best to confront Chen with what I knew. Suppose he lost control of himself? Suppose he physically attacked me? Suppose he saw nothing for it but to shut me up, as they say? There were a number of things in the dining room – chairs, vases, candlesticks – that could be used as blunt instruments. I saw him before me, I could hear what he'd say: 'So you've thought far enough to pinpoint me as a terrorist – but not far enough to work out that, to a terrorist, one victim more or less probably doesn't mean much. You don't think I'm going to let you simply walk out of here and wreck my entire organisation, do you?'

And then what? Chen was ten years younger than me, and a good deal stronger and quicker off the mark.

Alexi came out of the kitchen with a tea-towel, stopped by the bar, dried his hands and said, 'All done and dusted, boss. Would you like me to come in an hour early this evening? Then we could get that ivy out of the way before we start serving dinner.'

I hesitated. 'No, Alexi, it can wait until tomorrow.'

'Okay.' He tapped his forehead. 'See you later, and have a nice afternoon.'

'Thanks, Alexi. You too,'

After he'd left, I went to close the front door, took out my telephone and called Chen.

'Yes?'

'Just calling to say lunch is ready.'

'What luck. Here I was even boasting to everyone: my partner wants to wring my neck, but first he'll wine and dine me at the incomparable Chez Max. Well, I know where my priorities lie.'

I jumped. 'You were boasting about it?'

Chen sighed. 'Joke, Max, joke! Since when do we go around proclaiming that we even exist? I'll be with you in half an hour. And don't forget: I want to know the truth.'

The truth, I thought as I put my phone back in my jacket pocket. Why did he of all people keep talking about the truth? How had that café owner quoted Chen yesterday? 'A truth, or your truth – but *the* truth, what nonsense.' And there, just for once, he was right. Could my truth be his as well?

As I took a table out into the courtyard and put it down near the barbecue, I was thinking: even if he admits everything we're still worlds apart. Even if he doesn't deny the facts – there was, after all, a kind of moral truth. And if he had ever known what that was, how could he have come around to organizing suicide bombings?

I laid the table, stuck the bug under its surface, opened a bottle of Franken wine and went into the kitchen to warm up the sauerkraut. Then I sat down near the glazed door again, poured myself more white wine, and looked up at the walls now clear of ivy. No one living in the rest of the building had a view down into the courtyard. When I had the former laundry converted to make it a restaurant, Ashcroft got me an order whereby all windows looking out on the yard must be bricked up. Otherwise I could hardly have put any tables outside without disturbing people. There were protests at first, of course, but after the first tenants were taken to court for rebuilding their living-room without a permit and in a manner calculated to offend against the Protection of Historic Monuments law, the others soon calmed down.

My eyes went to the barbecue. As I laid the table, I'd seen the handle of the axe in passing. Of course I hoped fervently it wouldn't come to that, but if Chen really did run amok, I had a means of self-defence handy.

Ten minutes later there was a knock at the front door.

★

'Are we on a date or something?' Chen looked from the elegantly laid, flower-bedecked table in the courtyard to me and winked. 'I thought we were more likely to be at daggers drawn, and all this time you've been wanting to marry me!'

'I just thought this was an important moment, and so …'

'Sure. Getting married is a very important moment indeed.'

'I thought we had a few things to clear up, so I tried to create a suitable setting.'

'What, in this courtyard?'

'Why not? It's such a lovely day. And don't worry, no one can hear us.'

'I'm not worrying.' He looked sceptically at me. 'But you look just the way I imagine someone who is shitting their pants.'

Then he went out into the courtyard, over to the heap of ivy, and looked around. I stayed by the door.

'Would you like an aperitif? Or shall I get our lunch at once?'

Ignoring my question, he pointed to the ivy and asked, 'Is that by any chance my funeral pyre?'

'Oh, please, Chen! Do be serious for once!'

'Serious?' He raised his glance from the ivy and looked sharply at me. 'Very well then – let's be serious. Seriously then, this whole thing looks like you've set a trap for me. No staff on the premises, key turned twice in the lock of the front door, no one who can see or hear us here, and a man who's already unsuccessful anyway and must now be afraid he'll be informed on to his superior. Apart from all the rest of it … after all, there has to be some reason why you, having done hardly anything recently as an Ashcroft agent, start investigating me. You must have quite a backlog of resentment there?'

'I've no idea what you're …'

'Oh, come off it!' He sighed, and said wearily, 'Let's not have any more of this stupid stuff.' Then he raised his eyebrows in an exaggerated way, and shook his head as if rhetorically. 'What, no years of fury with your clod of a partner? No jealousy, no envy? No constant feeling that you're more upright, better behaved, more correct in general, but it still doesn't pay off? Not even with women, in fact least of all with them. They'd rather go out with your clod of a partner. I saw you filming Natalia with your sexomat shooter. Incidentally, I would dislike it very much if we were to get into bed with the same woman, however indirectly …'

'I was only filming her to …'

'I don't want to know why you did it,' he interrupted me. 'I just want you to know I saw you. Let's hope you remember that when you get into the suit, and let's hope it will spoil the idea of Natalia for you and you'll feed some other woman into the simulator.'

I moved out into the yard myself, went over to the table and poured wine from the squat bottle. 'Sure you wouldn't like a drink before we eat?'

'No, I would not like a drink. I'd like to know what's going on around here.'

'Don't get so worked up,' I replied, perhaps a little too energetically. But what on earth was he thinking of? When I'd gone to all that trouble with the table and the meal! 'Let's have a glass of wine together. And if you really distrust me …' Suppressing my fury, I took off my jacket at a deliberately leisurely pace. 'Here, look, all clean, no weapon, no trap.'

Chen stopped short and then shook his head incredulously. 'Well, if I didn't distrust you before, then I definitely
do now. Maybe I need that drink after all.'

He came towards me, and I could sense the tension in
him. As if he were ready to leap at me any moment. I
wondered briefly whether to raise my glass to him, but
then I was afraid my hand might shake.

Chen drank without taking his eyes off me.

When he put the glass down on the table again, he said,
'Right. We've had a glass of wine together. Now do I
finally get an explanation?'

I put my hand in my trouser pocket and switched the
bug on. At the same time I glanced to one side briefly,
checking my distance from the barbecue. Chen was about
five metres away from me. Was it his sweat I could smell?

I heard myself say huskily, 'I know about you.'

Chen put his head to one side and opened his mouth
as if we were in some comedy show. I'd seen him assume
that expression so often. Always when something really
mattered to me.

'Oh yes?' he said casually. 'So what about it?'

We looked each other in the eye, and I suddenly felt my
head was empty. And then it was anything but. My whole
body felt as if it were on some kind of rack. All the same
I knew this must go on, I must bring this business to an
end. There was no going back.

My words sounded as if I'd learnt them by heart. 'I
know you're a terrorist. You plan assassinations, you hide
Iranians, no one except for suicide bombers comes out of
Iran …' I stopped and took a deep breath. Chen was still
staring fixedly at me. 'And you've managed to hide for
years behind the things you say, because of course no one
ever thought that someone in conflict with our society

would proclaim his hatred so openly. For instance, those Iranians ...'

'The Iranians,' he interrupted me in a loud voice, although I registered a slight tremor in it, 'are refugees! Deserters from the Iranian army. The father of the family refused to go to a training camp for ...'

'Oh, Chen! Stop it, for goodness' sake!' And suddenly I let fly. It all poured out of me. 'Stop telling your lying tales! I've seen through you! You're a danger! A subversive! An enemy of the system! A terrorist living a life of luxury! Women and whisky and planting bombs on the side! And then there's your alleged success rate! You've probably just been hauling poor innocent souls before the courts over the years so that no one would get on your trail! Super-Chen! You of all people! You arrogant, spoilt bastard! You don't know anything about human beings! I'm going to look into all your cases, and then we'll see how many innocent men and women you've sent to labour camps! As if you could ever predict crimes in advance! You have to like human beings for that, you have to be able to put yourself in their place! And what can you do? You despise them, make them look small and ridiculous, nothing more!'

I was struggling for air. Chen had retreated a metre or so, and his face was strangely distorted, by fury as much as by fear. Of course! What else? I had him by the throat!

He said, 'I'm going now. You're right, I don't particularly like you, and very likely it's a fact that I can't put myself in your place, but I can see that you'd like to murder me. And do you know something?' He took another step back. 'This is a case for the Ashcroft agency. *You* are the danger. You're a crazed fanatic. You ought not to be on the loose.'

I laughed as I had never heard myself laugh before. This was total lunacy! Was I the fanatic? Was I the murderer?

And to show even more clearly how mad he was, I laughed. 'Ha ha ha! Ho, ho! Ha ha ha!'

He turned to the glazed door.

'Stay here, you bastard! We still have things to discuss!'

He turned his head to look at me, and once again I could see the fear in his face. I felt immense satisfaction. Let him crawl to me, the swine!

'Stay where you are,' he said tonelessly. 'You're over-excited. I'm going to send someone along to help you. Try to calm down. Drink another glass of wine. And don't try following me. I'll climb out through the window. It's all okay – maybe you're simply a little overwrought …'

So he was advising me to drink another glass of wine, was he? What did he think this was, just a heated argument? No, this was good against evil! This was … And suddenly the scales seemed to fall from my eyes … *We will crush the motherfuckers before they crush us!* Yes, I'll crush him! I want to crush him! I would love to crush him! It's necessary to crush him! He will not crush me!

And as Chen was still looking at me anxiously, but at the same time almost imploringly, I stepped back and reached behind the barbecue for the handle of the axe.

The rest was merely a kind of choreography. As if I'd been rehearsing what followed for years. Every move was right, every step was purposeful, everything was confined to what had to be done. I left no traces.

Some two hours later, when I let the rubbish bags drop into the Seine at a deserted place on the bank, it was as if I were ridding myself at a stroke of all the encumbrances of my life. As if my fears were sinking into the water before my eyes, all my pangs of conscience, all the injuries and humiliations, all the painful baggage of my life over the last few years. Suddenly I understood what people meant when they said they felt born again. Washed clean.

And even more important: I had done my duty. I was a worthy heir of John Ashcroft. The world was rid of Chen. And I had no doubt whatsoever that the world was now a better place.

Chapter 7

I spent the next few days partly in a state of euphoria, partly on tenterhooks. Because however carefully and conscientiously I had gone about it, of course there was always the possibility of a witness or some stupid coincidence. Suppose the bags with Chen in them were fished up by an angler, or found by one of the boats that dredged sludge out of the Seine? The brief time-span between his visit to Chez Max and the discovery of his remains would at least have raised questions.

So far as the Localization Office computer was concerned, and as long as the bags remained undiscovered, Chen was still moving around the eighth arrondissement, although on an erratic course. Near Natalia's apartment I had attached his transmitter to the collar of a dog tied up outside a food store. I naturally put it down to chance that the first dog I saw with no one watching it happened to be a Pekinese. Well, to chance in one way. In another – and I am far from being a religious man – perhaps there was someone up there after all playing games with Fate. In any event, I thought on the way back to Chez Max, this is exactly the kind of joke that Chen enjoys – that Chen would have enjoyed, I corrected myself. I had to grin. He would certainly have appreciated the humour of it, and I was glad I knew that and thought it as funny as he would. I even imagined us sitting together, both of us laughing at it.

Only that night, as my tension subsided, did the first unsettling questions come into my mind. Had I perhaps been seen from the other side of the river? Would one of my staff notice the dark stains on the terracotta tiles paving the courtyard? I hadn't been able to get them out in spite of repeated scrubbing. Or would someone notice the absence of a few ornamental stones which I'd taken from the fountain behind the barbecue to weight the bags?

However, my fears were unfounded. Nothing happened for the next three days. I even went to Ashcroft Central Office twice to pick up any information I could about Chen. I was expecting something like, 'Can you tell me where Wu is? I was supposed to be meeting him yesterday.' Or: 'You can tell your partner that Youssef has been trying to reach him for the last two days, and he's not very happy about it.' But no one said anything of the kind. Nor was anyone behaving oddly to me, avoiding me in the corridor or looking away when our eyes met. I had twice in the past seen what it was like when almost all agents except the man concerned knew he'd soon be coming before the Ashcroft tribunal for some offence or other. As if a dead man were walking around the building, and as if death was infectious.

But it seemed as if, at least for now, Chen's last appearance in this world had been with that drop into the Seine and the bubbles that rose from him.

On the fourth day I called Commander Youssef at about eleven in the morning and told him I'd been trying to get hold of Chen for four days, but his phone was either switched off or still out of order, and up to yesterday evening the Localization Office had given me only some very odd locations for him, and he hadn't stayed long in any of them: dog-exercising areas in public parks, pavements outside butchers' shops, and according to the data found on the Ashcroft computer, an apartment belonging to a gay electrician.

'... Anyway, Chen – or I suppose it must be Chen – was nowhere around when I went to look for him in the places the Localization Office gave me. And I didn't want to ring the electrician's doorbell because ... well, as far as I know there's nothing wrong with the electricity in Chen's apartment at the moment, and even if there were ... I mean, why an electrician from the eighth arrondissement?'

Youssef muttered something which, in him, sounded like laughter. 'That would be quite something! Chen an Illy boy!'

'A what?'

'Oh, come on, Schwarzwald ... everyone knows about them. Because of the coffee. Never seen it? Buy&Help: uterus implants for men. The coffee, you must know about it. It tastes ... well, it doesn't taste so good.'

'Sorry, Commander, I always have a kind of uneasy feeling about the Buy&Help campaigns. Of course most of it is in a good cause, but still ... well, it's really just a sales stunt.'

'Hmhm ... yes. Well, what did you want to know about Chen for?'

'To be honest, Commander, I'm worried.'

'Worried about Chen? You'd do better to be worrying a little more about yourself.'

'I know, Commander, my success rate ...'

'Your success rate?' he interrupted me. 'You don't have any successes to your credit. Except for your friend the painter.'

I felt as if some kind of sour acid were running right through me.

'Well, I'm working on various cases which I hope will soon lead to results.'

'I hope so too. Right: why are you worried about Chen, then?'

'Commander …' I took a deep breath, making it audible to him '… for one thing I believe I found out at last, yesterday evening, what's behind Chen's walks around the eighth arrondissement. His transmitter is on a dog's collar. I wasn't able to check that myself, because the dog's owner was always with the animal, but the data from the Localization Office and the locations of the dog on three occasions matched exactly, to the nearest metre. Then it occurred to me that I'd seen the dog a few days before while searching for Chen, only at first I naturally didn't connect them. What's more, if Chen wanted to get rid of his transmitter and disappear without trace – you know his sense of humour – well, the dog in question is a Pekinese. And unfortunately that all matches my assumption that Chen has made off somewhere.'

'Made off? How do you mean?' That amused sound again. 'To that Illy poof?'

Not for the first time, I was conscious of Youssef's origins: a man from the suburbs, an Arab – who else would allow himself to speak of people of a different sexual orientation like that? It probably took more than four or five generations to get the desert right out of an Arab's mind.

'No, that's not what I meant,' I said rather sharply. 'I meant that perhaps Chen has gone to the other side of the Fence.'

'What …? What puts that into your head?'

Once again I drew an audible breath before I told

148

Youssef about the Iranian illegals under surveillance by the TFSP, and how annoyed Chen had been about it. 'I've never seen him like that before. And you know Chen: he can lose his temper over all sorts of things, but he's always in perfect control of himself at work. Nothing really impresses him. So when he fell into such a rage because the TFSP was watching them, I began to feel suspicious, and I stuck close to him one evening.'

'You shadowed your partner?'

'Well, Commander, partner or no partner … I mean, Lieutenant Gilbert made it quite clear that there was something wrong about Chen and the illegals in the Rue de la Roquette.'

He didn't reply. Because he hadn't read the last few days' reports accumulating in his computer? Because he preferred studying interior design websites to choose curtains or tiles for his villa in Perpignan? What had Chen said? *A pretty wife and two more years to go before he retires?* The fact was, there was a certain irony in Youssef's blaming me for my low success quota. In-house, we all knew that recently he'd hardly been killing himself with overwork.

Anyway, he didn't seem to have read the email that Lieutenant Gilbert or Self-Protection must have sent him to inform him, as Chen's superior officer, of their suspicion that Chen might be involved in something shady. One-nil to me or against him, whichever way you liked to see it.

'… And in fact, at the beginning anyway, I naturally followed him hoping it was all some mistake. Because one thing seemed logical to me: if there was really anything in what the TFSP suspected, then Chen was sure to react quickly. So I thought if I kept an eye on him, saw him going out for a meal after finishing work in the normal way, meeting friends or so on, then that, luckily, would settle it in his favour.'

'No need to keep on making out that you're so anxious about whatever's happened to Chen. You aren't exactly bosom friends.'

'Commander, if I may say so: Chen has his faults, and working with him certainly isn't always easy, but I have the greatest respect for him as an Ashcroft man, and I wouldn't want to exchange him for anyone else as my partner – or more precisely I wouldn't have wanted to until four days ago.'

'All right, come to the point, Schwarzwald.'

Were the interior design catalogues waiting?

I cleared my throat. 'Well, sure enough, I saw him eating with a girlfriend, at work with his gardening, although – and it's hard for me to say this about my partner; I mean, after four years of working together – ' I was happy to keep him impatient. 'Although he twice met terrorists known to us, once in the back room of a Vietnamese take-away, and then right outside the door of his building. Of course he had to expect surveillance by the TFSP, that's probably why he linked his meetings with an evening otherwise spent perfectly innocently.'

'Terrorists …?' All of a sudden there was considerable uneasiness in Youssef's voice. No wonder: a colleague of ours connected with terrorism – that was bad enough for the superior officer concerned, but it was much worse if the said superior officer had never expressed any passing suspicion to his own superiors. Because he wasn't really interested in what went on in his own department any more. Because instead of keeping an eye on his agents he preferred to study illustrations of marble tiles. That could mean early and far from honourable departure from his post, which in its own turn would lead to reductions in his pension payments.

In short: I had been correct in working out, over the last few days, that it would hardly be in Youssef's own interests to make Chen's disappearance into any big deal.

'I've taken photographs of the men and fed them into our computer …'

And I gave him the names of two terrorists who, according to our information, were hiding out in Paris. The photos really existed. They were on the desk in front of me; I'd drawn them up from the computer.

'Well … I don't know, Schwarzwald, all this sounds rather bizarre to me …'

He was sounding positively subdued for someone in his position. Sometimes it was better not to have any results. The commander of the Ashcroft agents in the eleventh arrondissement wasn't going to get any commendation for this one, at least.

'I mean, Chen is a crazy guy, but …'

'Look, Commander, I've been thinking a lot over the last few days about Chen and the way he so often talked. And you know that his language … well, it's no secret that he sometimes didn't shrink from … let's say, verging on taboo subjects. And the logical consequence of that …'

'Oh, this is nonsense! Chen talks big, and we indulge him, that's all. He likes to think he knows all about everything that's wrong with the world, but when all's said and done he'd rather be sitting in the warm toasting his feet.'

'I'm sorry, Commander, but … for instance, I remember him saying that – well, as he rather abruptly put it, too much fuss is made about getting things. And then he blamed the Enlightenment, and words like understanding and knowledge and so on – well, to me that means clearly that he was always convinced that deeds must follow words at some point.'

'Of course he was convinced of it – only not *his* deeds. Chen is a clever man and also – between you and me – a randy goat, and he knows he won't change the world and he has only one life. That doesn't mean he wouldn't happily support someone else, someone he sees as more just or more moral, who took over, but until then … And what's more …' I could see him before me, shaking his head in disbelief. 'What's more, Chen is my best man! How many of our colleagues who may be as loyal as anything to the state and the law but are total washouts wouldn't I give for him!'

Like me, for example, I thought. You puffed-up goat-fucker!

'Oh, I understand how you feel, Commander. It was a great shock to me too. Only when I thought it over later … listen, I think we'd better just wait for now. Perhaps Chen will turn up again; perhaps that business with the dog is just a practical joke. Perhaps he wants to fool the ladies in the Localization Office, something like that. And it can't be ruled out that he could have got in touch with the terrorists in the course of an investigation. Then if he doesn't turn up … well, you have my word for it that I won't kick up a great fuss. We could always say Chen has simply gone missing. These things do happen, after all.'

I could hear him breathing hard, and I knew what an effort it cost him to say, 'Okay, Schwarzwald, I think I really would be grateful if you'd keep quiet about Chen's meetings with the terrorists for the time being. As you very sensibly suggest, let's wait and see.'

★

And that was just what happened. We waited. Over the following weeks and months, several explanations of Chen's disappearance were suggested. Some of our colleagues thought he had fallen foul of the whisky and the Scottish moors; others, the more romantic souls among us, usually women, felt sure that a love affair had taken him to the other side of the Fence; others again, supplied by me with hints, thought he knew that Self-Protection was after him for hiding illegals and so he had no option but to go underground. At least, the bags containing his remains never came to light.

Two weeks after my phone call to Youssef I got a new partner. He was useless, certainly compared to Chen, and in other ways too. His success quota was regularly below average, his cover was working as a car-park attendant, he lived on lettuce and high-energy bars – which was a joke when you thought of his uninspired lack of energy at work – he had a wife he didn't love and they went camping on Narbonne beach once a year, he smelled strongly of perfume, and he picked his nose throughout our discussions. But it worked on me like a rejuvenation cure. I positively blossomed as an Ashcroft agent. Suddenly I could see and sense what was going on in my area again, within a single week I brought two forgers of brand-name goods, one terrorist sympathizer and even a potential murderer before the Examining Committee, and I basked in the renewed appreciation of my colleagues. It felt wonderful, after four years of humiliation, to be Number One in the team again.

I strolled around the eighth arrondissement without any particular plan in mind a few times, and one afternoon, by chance, I came upon Natalia in a tea-room. I sat down at the next table and made several attempts to strike up a conversation with her. Did she come here often, hadn't we met before … But obviously she was one of those women who thought, because of the way they looked, they could treat other people less well endowed by nature like bothersome flies – at least, unless those other people were loud-mouthed Asians. Well, next morning I was ashamed of it, but I couldn't help myself that night. What was it she had said to me? 'Monsieur, even if we really have met before, you are not someone I would remember. Would you please let me drink my tea in peace?'

And she had sounded as grave, almost piously so, as if she were looking down on me from some planet which concerned itself with the really important things in life.

Such arrogance! And how ridiculous she had made me look in front of the other customers. All the way home I felt kind of soiled. And so I had to give it to her. As I said, I was ashamed of it in the morning, and even that night I felt a kind of moral void in me when I brought out the sexomat suit from behind the sofa. On the other hand the times when I had let people treat me like dirt were finally over. I wasn't taking that kind of thing from the likes of Chen's ex-girlfriend – or, if you like, from Chen himself.

Incidentally, I would dislike it very much if we were to get into bed with the same woman, however indirectly.

Well, too bad about that!

And then something happened that showed the events of the last few weeks in an entirely different light.

In the middle of June I received a letter from Paris

Central Penitentiary. (I suppose prisons were the only places where letters were still written, since for security reasons the inmates weren't allowed to use the Internet or send emails.)

The letter was from Leon, and I snatched it out of my post box with great excitement and sat down on the stairs inside the hall of the restaurant to read it.

Dear Max

Forgive me for not getting in touch for so long, but what happened, as you can imagine, was a bad shock. I'm not sure how much people know about my crime in our part of town, and above all how much you know. When I was, well, let's say being driven away by the police in that new miracle vehicle, I could see you through the window. You looked dismayed and helpless, and I felt really sorry. What must you have imagined, what terrible crimes had I been committing behind your back over the years of our friendship? But the fact is they picked me up for one thing because of the smoking, and of course you knew about that, but also because of a totally stupid plan to deal in drugs. I was just about washed up, financially too, and for a few weeks it seemed to me a way out of my dilemma. Ah well, we're not immune to outright nonsense even in our mid-thirties. Of course I wonder who gave me away – although I'm pretty sure it was the Arab who first suggested the drug-dealing to me and indeed persuaded me into it, probably in order to bargain with the police over something else. But I wonder not because, as I expect you're thinking, I was furious with whoever turned me in or even wanted revenge, quite the opposite. The funny thing is – and you are reading this quite correctly! – I'm grateful to him. Grateful? More than that – he saved my life! Because shall I tell you something? Believe it or not, I've started painting again in prison! After only two weeks I was doing little pencil drawings, and then my uncle sent me paints, brushes and a small easel, and now I sit for four to six hours every day, just as I used to, painting picture after picture. The deputy governor in charge of this wing is very enthusiastic, he brings me fresh fruit and flowers for my still lifes every few days, and has got me excused from the usual work you have to do in jail. In return I give him a picture a week, and he tells me how he and his family, wife, parents-in-law, three adolescent children, take time off every evening to listen to classical music and do nothing but look at my latest work. Isn't that wonderful? Isn't it a dream?

So you'll understand that almost nothing could have been better for me. My arrest, the prison sentence, the grey, bleak atmosphere here, the terrible food – I often think of you, and God knows I wouldn't say no to a plate of your Königsberg meatballs now – the hard mattresses, the awful light, the smell of my fellow prisoners, their dreary conversation – well, all that was the shot in the arm that I needed to break free of my artist's block, my state of lethargic depression. I'm back! There's wholegrain pasta and courgette puree for lunch, the others are all talking about fucking, some kind of downmarket pop music, all thud, thud, is coming through the loudspeakers as it does all the time, everywhere – and I feel happy. Because back in my cell my easel is waiting for me.

So, my dear friend, at last I have news for you. Naturally I'd be very glad if you answered, but don't go to any trouble.

See you – well, not so very soon (they gave me three years, two with good conduct, anyway time enough to prepare for several exhibitions), but see you sometime. And warm good wishes from your friend,
Leon.

I dropped my hand holding the letter, and stared into space for a while. There were tears in my eyes. At that moment I could hardly have imagined better news.

It was as if Fate had at long last patted me on the shoulder and said, 'You have trodden your own path in the face of all obstacles and all doubts, you have done your duty. In spite of betraying your best friend, you did not weaken, but on the contrary you drew from that the energy you needed to see the truth about your Ashcroft partner clearly at long last. You freed society from Chen, and in the end you saved your friend's life, as he himself says. Well done, Max, all credit to you, you're a remarkable guy.'

I didn't move until Ravelli came into the hall about half an hour later, on his way to prepare for lunch. When he saw me sitting on the dimly lit stairs near the back door of Chez Max, he said in surprise, 'Morning, boss. Everything all right?'

I looked up. I was probably smiling as happily as a drunk. 'Oh yes, Ravelli, everything's all right.' And then I pointed my forefinger at him. 'I tell you what, we'll serve champagne today, and the bubbly will be on the house!'

'Wow!' Ravelli looked intrigued for a moment, and then he grinned. 'Did the fox by any chance find his vixen?'

'No, not that, Ravelli, but the fox has found himself again. Here,' I said, slapping myself on the chest, 'he's found himself again in here. He has what matters to him back, he's himself again. He's a happy fox!'

'Ah,' said Ravelli, hesitating. Which made sense, because how could he understand. 'Well, that sounds great.'

I nodded and said, folding up Leon's letter and putting it in my shirt pocket, 'It doesn't just sound great, Ravelli, it *is* great.'

And then we went into the kitchen of Chez Max, and I helped him to open the oysters for the first course.